The Dance of the Rose

A Novel

Based on a true story

Includes over two dozen testimonies.

Betty Viamontes

The Dance of the Rose

Published in the United States by Zapote Street Books, LLC, Tampa, Florida

This book is a work of fiction. Characters, names, places, events, incidents, and businesses are either a product of the author's imagination or used fictitiously. Any resemblance to actual locales or events, or to any persons, living or dead, is entirely coincidental.

ISBN: 978-0-986423765

Book cover photo by Betty Viamontes

Printed in the United States of America

I dedicate this book—

To my mother, a rose against a backdrop of the dilapidated houses on Zapote Street, a master of invention, hope in the face of misery.

To Aunt Pilar and Uncle Mario, for their love, kindness, and selflessness.

To my husband, Ivan, for finding me when I needed to be found.

To my readers, for making my books part of their permanent collections.

Chapter 1 - At Sea

I NEVER CONSIDERED myself a normal girl—awkward, impulsive, unpredictable, intelligent, introspective, pathetic, perhaps, but not normal—and no matter how hard I tried, I did not fit neatly into any group.

As the oldest of my siblings, I often found myself defending or caring for my little brother, Gustavo, like on the day of my twelfth birthday, when he fell on the porch while holding a glass of water. The glass hit the red tile, shattering into tiny pieces, and Gustavo's hands landed on them. The thin nine-year-old, who looked younger than his age, with brown hair and beautiful, big brown eyes, cried inconsolably as he showed me his bloody hands, sprinkled with encrusted pieces of glass. When this occurred, the three adults who lived in our house—my mother, Laura; Aunt Berta; and Uncle Antonio—were all at work. Despite my fear of blood, I poured some sugar over his wounds, carefully removed as many pieces of glass as I could and rinsed his hands thoroughly. After pressing clean towels over his cuts, I collected a group of kids from the neighborhood who volunteered to accompany me, and we rode a bus to the emergency room of the closest hospital.

When our turn to be seen arrived, the doctor shrank his eyebrows once he noticed the group of boys and girls.

"Where is his mother?" he asked.

"I'm his oldest sister," I said. "My mother cannot be reached at work because she is out all day collecting money from grocery stores. We won't see her again until tonight. I didn't want my brother to bleed out."

"How old are you?" he asked.

"Twelve," I said with conviction.

Even if it had occurred to me to contact Aunt Berta or Uncle Antonio at work when Gustavo fell, we did not have a telephone at home, as only those with ties to the communist party, for the most part, had one. Every time my mother needed to call my father, who lived in Miami, she used a neighbor's telephone. I imagined that after a few years, our neighbor must have regretted offering the use of her telephone in the first place, but who would have thought that when my father left our home in Havana in 1968, with the idea of reuniting with us in the United States shortly after, it would take twelve years before we would see him again?

My name is Tania. My sister, Lynette, was a year younger than me and two years older than my brother, but my stick figure caused some people to conclude that my sister was the oldest.

As we grew up and turned into teenagers, I never envied Lynette's more developed chest, because for some reason, boys seemed attracted to me. I wondered why, when, in addition to her fuller figure, Lynette's laughter and innate happiness could light up a room, while I acted more serious and reserved.

Chapter 1 - At Sea

My idea of fun consisted of making up stories in my head and reducing them to paper on an old typewriter that my mother's students used to practice typing. I also liked to memorize the long names of chemical compounds.

My childhood had been marked by a series of defining events or situations: growing up without my father, witnessing my mother's attempted suicide when I was six, and coping with the night terrors when I feared she would do it again.

On the day she attempted to take her own life, shortly after the government told her that she would never be able to leave Cuba to reunite with my father, I arrived from school just in time. As I walked through the house calling her, my ponytail swung from side to side and the white blouse of my red-and-white uniform stuck to my sweaty back. Drops of perspiration rolled down my face when I found her, standing in the middle of the room, her hair and dress soaking wet. It took me a few seconds to understand what was about to happen, but then adrenaline kicked in. I ran to her, removed the matches from her hand and rushed outside for help.

That was the first time I saved her, but life or destiny would allow me to save her on two more occasions. The last would be the most difficult. People in Cuba believed in destiny, which made me wonder whether, since the day of my birth, it had been predisposed that I would be present at the precise moments when she would need me the most.

During my years living in Cuba, the closest I came to feeling normal was on my fifteenth birthday; the day, in which—according to Cuban tradition—I transitioned from childhood to adulthood. My mother threw the biggest party our neighborhood had seen, a party people would talk about for years after we eventually left. The embarrassing pimples that emerged on my face at the age of thirteen had been virtually eliminated by multiple and painful treatments at the Koayam Beauty Salon in Galiano Street, located in the neighborhood of Centro Habana. My mother paid a fortune for these treatments. She wanted to give me a birthday to remember, and that, she accomplished.

She asked the neighbor who had the most beautiful colonial-style house in the neighborhood if she could use her courtyard, a spacious area where the neighbor taught Spanish dancing, for my celebration. The courtyard had a separate entrance and elaborate tile floors that, despite the age of the house, maintained the luster of bygone years.

My father sent me two of the dresses I wore that night—one of a floral print fabric (black with red roses), spaghetti straps, and layers of ruffles; the second one of a lightweight beige fabric that draped like a waterfall. His package also included fabric for two more dresses: orange-and-silver *lamé* and off-white muslin. My boyfriend and I stood on the porch when the package arrived from the United States, two months before my birthday. I anxiously opened it, and my eyes lit up when I saw its contents.

"I can't wait to dance with you on your birthday," he said. "You will look beautiful."

But I would not dance with him on that particular evening. Mother insisted I had to dance with a boy who owned a suit. She wanted to send pictures to my father, and they had to be perfect, so she found the most unlikely of suitors: the son of a Communist Party member.

People in the neighborhood whispered when they saw me: "The daughter of a *gusano* dancing with the son of a Communist Party member? How does that happen?" The answer was simple. Everyone, even the communists, wanted to be part of the biggest party of the year, so the

Communist Party member asked to be invited. Mother refused at first, but the official seemed relentless.

"I will provide security and all the drinks for the party," he said. "Also, my son may dance with your daughter for the pictures. He owns a nice suit, and I heard you were looking for someone who had one."

"Can he just lend the suit to my daughter's boyfriend?"

"It won't fit. My son is shorter."

My mother thought about it. She knew her life could become even more difficult if she did not invite him. In that case, why not get something out of him? She took a deep breath.

"He will only dance with her during the choreography, and I will be watching him closely. He will keep his distance from my daughter. She is *not* for sale."

"Understood," he said.

Later that day, when my mother shared the story with Aunt Berta, she raised her eyebrows and opened her eyes wide.

"How do you dare negotiate with people like that?" Aunt Berta asked.

That was my mother: a master of invention, always finding a way; a rose against the backdrop of the unpainted, deteriorated colonial houses on Zapote Street. Hope in the face of misery.

To save money for the party, Mother had worked over twelve hours a day for years: from eight to noon at the grocery stores, and from noon to four teaching adult students in an improvised classroom close to our house. She would give assignments to her students, run home to set up the typewriters, and return to the classroom after assigning the typing lessons to the three or four people she taught. Then, from four to eight in the evening, she would work at the grocery stores again.

On weekends, Mother sold goods in the black market: vegetables she bought illegally from a farmer in Güira de Melena, one of Havana's countryside towns, and eye pencils people thought my father had sent from the United States. She believed that the man who sold them to her had made them out of stolen materials. After all, the government controlled everything. Many people rationalized stealing from the government with the Cuban saying: "Thief who steals from thief has one hundred years of forgiveness." They believed that when the Castro government nationalized all industry and means of production, shortly after the triumph of the revolution in 1959, the government had stolen from the people, who now felt justified in doing the same.

For my *quince* celebration, my mother masterfully managed every detail: the swans that decorated my cake, the photographers, the music, the father-and-daughter dance where my uncle Antonio fulfilled the role of my father. The owner of the house where my party was held allowed us to use her formal dining room for the cake and her master bedroom for some of the pictures.

So, there I was, in my long, white muslin dress —my light brown hair falling in curls over my shoulders, my nails freshly painted pink—dancing with the son of a Communist Party member, while my boyfriend stood within the crowd and watched. I kept looking at him. "I'm so sorry," I whispered.

Later, my sister told me that I looked like an aristocrat from pre-communist years, like those we had seen in old movies, with my ivory skin and professional makeup that made me look prettier than I was. My neck smelled of a flowery perfume Aunt Berta brought home as a gift from a Russian woman whose house she had designed.

Like everyone else in Cuba, Aunt Berta worked for the government, but she could not tell anyone about the nature of her job. She told me the government did not want people to know that while the houses of the Cubans were crumbling, Russians could enjoy new homes.

Other than not being able to dance with my boyfriend that evening, I loved my fifteenth birthday celebration. My mother had successfully showed me what it felt like to feel normal for once, even to feel like Cinderella—except that back then, I did not appreciate or understand all it took to arrange such a celebration in a place where people hardly had enough to eat.

But my taste of "normal" did not last.

A few weeks after my birthday, a group of Cubans drove a bus through the gates of the Peruvian Embassy in Havana, killing a guard. Embassy officials refused to turn in the offenders, and as retribution, the Castro government removed security from the entrance. In no time, over ten thousand people had flooded the embassy to request political asylum. They were tired of the living conditions in Cuba: the meager rations, the deteriorated infrastructure, the lack of freedom. Castro knew he needed to let some steam off the pressure-cooker Cuba had become. A massive exodus was his solution.

After Castro's announcement that those with relatives in the United States who wanted to leave could do so if their relatives came to pick them up by boat, my mother secretly called my father and told him: "Hurry, there's no time to lose. This is our chance." She did not tell my siblings and me about the call because she wanted to protect us from the harassment that those choosing to abandon Cuba suffered.

The night before the guards came for us, I kissed my boyfriend goodbye on the porch under the watchful eyes of my mother, who monitored our every move through the bedroom window. That would be our last kiss.

After that night, my world would collapse into a vortex. The government officials did not allow us to take anything that reminded us of home, not even a change of clothes, and over the next few days, I learned what it was like to live in hell. First, the concentration camp–where we spent days eating little or no food, drinking water from a rusted faucet, taking turns at sleeping on a chair, being accosted by police dogs and heavily armed soldiers, watching my mother's desperation–and then the boat. That night, the guards stuffed over two hundred of us on a shrimp boat headed for the United States.

It was April 26, 1980, two months after my fifteenth birthday.

Not long after our boat left the port, gale-force winds and heavy rain started, and roughly thirty minutes later, I heard a male voice through loudspeakers:

"Attention, attention. This is the Cuban Coast Guard. There is a boat similar to this one nearby, and it's taking on water! It carries over two hundred men, women, and children onboard. If you see it, do what you can. That is all!"

I looked in the direction from where the voice was coming and noticed a small white powerboat next to our larger vessel. Beneath the yellow glow of the boat's light, an officer stood with a megaphone in his hand.

After the announcement, a mother held her daughter close to her bosom, a brother grabbed his younger sister's hand, a young couple embraced, and an old man took out a small stamp of the Virgin of Charity and prayed. Moments later, the coastguard's boat disappeared into the darkness, and from our ship's marine radio, we began to hear screams and calls for help. Our captain turned it off and announced:

"I'm sorry. There's nothing we can do. If we help them, we will seal our fate. Please, pray for them. I'm so sorry."

Chapter 1 - At Sea

My mother, my siblings, and I sat near the stern surrounded by men, women, and children who looked as scared as we felt. Mother asked my brother, my sister, and me to get closer to her and placed her arms around us. Her hands felt like ice, and her body trembled. After she huddled us together, guilt and fear paraded through her dark eyes.

"Please hold on to whatever you can," she said for the sake of saying something.

I could still hear the screams in my head and imagined the frantic fight of women and children to stay afloat. How many would needlessly die that night? How many relatives at home would never hear what happened to their loved ones? Would we be next?

Occasionally, our boat rose steeply with the waves and fell into the void they left. Other times, the sea smashed the port side relentlessly, creating a waterfall above our heads. I did not consider myself religious then, but in my thoughts, I asked God to keep our family safe.

When we lived in Cuba, my mother had taught us to believe in God even though the government frowned upon the practice of religion. As I grew up, every time I heard her cry in the middle of the night, I quietly asked him to care for her, to remove her sadness. It felt good to have something to believe in.

Some years later, my memories would block the screams I heard that evening, and my sister, who was thirteen years old when we left, would have to remind me that it had not been a bad dream.

Suddenly, the captain's voice redirected my attention as he stood on the hull:

"Listen up, everyone. I have an announcement to make." He paused for a moment, and all eyes focused on him. Although it was dark, the light of the boat allowed me to distinguish his imposing silhouette, but not his face.

"I went to Cuba to pick up my family and left with a boat full of strangers," he proceeded. "To the men taken out of jails tonight and forced to come with me, keep in mind there are many families here. If you dare to put a finger on them," he said touching his holster, "I will not hesitate to put a bullet in your head and throw you overboard. Is that clear?"

I swallowed and looked around us. Until then, I had not known that people released from the jails accompanied us. A group of shirtless men nearby nodded.

"The seas are choppy," he continued, "and they are about the get worse. Help women and children when they get sick. I will share the food and drinks I have with all of you. I know many of you have not eaten for several hours."

Following the announcement, the captain went back inside the cabin, and moments later, our ship began to rock more wildly than before—like a toy rising and falling with the waves' motion. I started to think about my father. Would I ever see him again? Would the long wait be in vain?

Everything I knew remained behind in Havana: my handful of friends, my journals, the old typewriter that had saved me from myself; my Spanish language, Aunt Berta and Uncle Antonio —who had been like my parents—and their two small daughters. My mother told us that this was the price we had to pay. "One day you will understand," she said.

As our boat danced wildly to the whims of the wind and the sea, I thought about Grandma. She had diabetes, and we had not seen her since we left Cuba as the captain had taken the sickest and oldest people inside the cabin to protect them from the elements. Grandma had already collapsed once during the days the government kept us at the concentration camp near the Port of Mariel. The long periods without eating caused her to have a seizure, less than forty eight hours after our arrival to the camp.

I scanned my surroundings. Vomit and rain flew around me, carried by the wind and the horizontal rain, and splashed my body and my clothes: a pair of green pants that were now too big on me after the days at the camp, and a white, sleeveless shirt that revealed my skeletal arms.

On one occasion, our boat tilted so much to one side that I feared a woman, a few feet away from me, would fall overboard. A couple of shirtless men rushed to her and grabbed her ankles right before we lost her. Chaos reigned around as sickened people rushed to the edge of the boat, while others, not finding the space, vomited on the deck.

Havana's lights had now disappeared, and the palms of my hands turned to ice as fear spread among us.

The captain gave orders to distribute soft drinks, except that none of the passengers knew how to open a can of Coke. His men tried to teach us, but some of us clumsily broke off the metal tab, and the captain's men had to open those cans with a small knife, a task difficult to accomplish during rough seas.

"Will Dad be waiting for us when we get to the United States?" my eleven-year-old brother asked Mom.

My brother had been affected by my father's absence more than my sister and me. Mother said that boys needed their dads, and in my brother's case, it was true. Unlike me, he never looked at Uncle Antonio as a father. My brother and Uncle Antonio were too different to connect intellectually or emotionally. My brother, like Dad, was good with his hands and cared little about reading, while Uncle Antonio never did any physical work and was always buried in the pages of engineering and history books.

Until that night, Uncle Antonio had been the only father I had known. He was six feet tall—one of the tallest men in our neighborhood—and had a full head of black hair that over the years had turned to salt-and-pepper. He personified the word "smart," from the glasses he only took off when he went to sleep to his incessant reading and theorizing. A neighbor told Aunt Berta that one day, as Uncle Antonio returned from his job as an engineer, a car almost ran him over because he crossed a street while reading a book. A second neighbor repeated the same story a year later.

I already missed Uncle Antonio.

For a moment, my attention turned to Gustavo, who was still waiting for my mother to respond to his question. His dark brown hair and clothes were soaked, and his narrow, skinny face looked shiny. My mother, who sat next to Gustavo, closed her eyes, massaged her neck with one hand, and tapped her index finger against her lap nervously.

"He doesn't know we left in another boat," she finally said. "So, no, I doubt he'll be there."

And how could he know? After my grandmother became ill at the camp, my mother managed to gain the compassion of one of the officers, and he allowed us to leave before it was our turn. Mom was afraid Dad would not believe the Cuban officers when his turn to pick us up arrived—back at the Port of Mariel, where hundreds of boats awaited—and he learned that we had already left. She hoped he would not do something he would regret.

Mother removed chunks of her wet, bleached hair from her face and tucked them behind her ears. Then, while she rubbed the back of her neck again, she noticed me looking at her. She reached for my head and caressed it gently. I didn't smile, just looked away.

I could taste the salt of the sea on my lips and hear the waves pounding our boat with so much force that sometimes I thought we did not stand a chance. Some people were still vomiting, but I was becoming numb to the smell.

I don't know how much time our boat struggled and strained against the sea; I could only hope for it to end.

Somehow, after a while, I fell asleep. When I awoke, not sure how long I had slept, I noticed that the darkness had left us and the sun was rising on the horizon. As my eyes focused in the distance where the blue sky kissed the sea, I did not distinguish land, only the gentle motion of calm waters. A couple of unfamiliar white birds flew above us, making me wonder if land was nearby.

Was I imagining the calm shades of blue around me? Was this what Heaven felt like? I breathed in the morning air and closed my eyes to enjoy the stillness, but my sister's familiar giggles made me aware that my surroundings were not of my imagination.

"What are you laughing at?" I asked.

"Your face and your clothes are caked in vomit. You look like a zombie."

My sister found comedy in every situation—a personality trait I wished I shared, but I always had a reason to be bitter, or rather, anxious; perhaps because I tended to over-analyze. While my sister relieved stress by laughing at situations, I was the eternal worrier, often fearful of what would happen next.

I glanced at my sister, my brother, and the people around us. We all looked the same way and smelled rotten. But the comfort of knowing we were safe made me forget about the way I looked or smelled and allowed me to doze off for a while longer.

My sleep was interrupted by the captain's voice coming out through the loudspeaker.

"Ladies and gentlemen. I need your attention, please," he said.

For the first time, I was able to have a clear view of the captain. Perhaps the way I recall him today is not how he looked, as time has a way of changing one's memories. I picture him as a tall, dark-haired man, a thick beard, tanned skin, and white teeth that sparkled like diamonds.

"There was a problem with the navigation," he said. "The land you see up there is not the United States. It's Cuba."

I looked up in the direction he was pointing and distinguished the first glimpses of land.

Following that statement, fear and confusion contorted people's faces. How could it be? We had been traveling for hours. My mother gave the captain an incredulous look, as if waiting for him to elaborate. Moments later, the captain made another announcement:

"I had you there for a moment! No, that is not Cuba. That land you see *is* the United States."

Families and strangers embraced and cried tears of happiness, while the captain smiled.

"It has been my pleasure to bring you to the land of the free, but I have a favor to ask you," he said.

The people focused their eyes on him, their faces blanketed with curiosity.

"When you get to America, never forget that my boat Capt. J.H. brought you to these lands. If there is anything I want you to remember about this night, remember the name of my boat."

I repeated that name to myself several times, to commit it to memory, although I was certain that no matter how many years would pass, the events of that night, the generosity of the captain, and the name of his boat would be ingrained in my mind forever.

Later, our boat would join the hundreds of boats full of people who were arriving in Key West. Red Cross workers, American soldiers, nuns, and other workers awaited our arrival and assisted us as we disembarked.

Grandma had to be taken out of the boat on a stretcher after the long night at sea.

"Welcome to America!" the soldiers, workers, and nuns would tell us with smiles on their faces.

The nuns gave us religious stamps, and one of them placed a crucifix on my grandmother's hand as her stretcher passed by. The Red Cross workers provided each passenger with a small bag containing toiletries. Some volunteers led us to an area filled with piles of donated used clothes, gave us each a large plastic bag, and told us to take as many clothes as we could fit in it.

A couple of hours later, Grandma joined us in the processing area. One of the workers brought her in a wheelchair to where we were. She was no longer pale as she was when I last saw her, and wore a donated beige dress. The worker gave my grandmother's bag of clothes to my mother. By then, we had been reunited with my father. His boat had arrived at Key West about an hour after ours did.

The warm reception my family received contrasted sharply with the vision I had of my new country. During my childhood, my teachers had portrayed the United States like a country that cared little for those less fortunate, but this welcome suggested a very different place, and validated my mother's perception, who had always portrayed the United States like a place where dreams come true.

A few days later, reality hit me as we walked on the streets of Miami with both of my parents, mesmerized and intimidated by our surroundings. We had a mountain to climb to achieve my mother's dreams. We did not speak English. My father, Rio, had not succeeded in this country during his years alone, and now, with more mouths to feed, I did not see how we could ever get ahead.

I had left part of me in Cuba. How could I replace Uncle Antonio, the only father I knew, for someone who hardly knew me? I appreciated all the years my father had waited for us, but I was not ready to let go of my past.

My mother, a woman in love with love, had big dreams for each one of us. It would take me years to understand her. Would my siblings and I be able to live up to her expectations? I also wondered if I would ever feel normal again.

Chapter 2 – The Beginning

From the moment I arrived in Miami, I suspected that my husband, Rio, was hiding something. He carried a concealed .45-caliber gun in a brown leather bag under his arm, and scanned his surroundings and the people around us, like a cheetah waiting for its prey.

Rio no longer looked like the man who'd left Cuba in 1968 with a full head of hair, a hopeful smile, and the conviction that he would see his three children and me again soon. Now, he had a cautious gaze and a receding hairline that revealed his temples' thick veins. Although, he remained thin, his muscular build, tanned skin, and tough-guy demeanor seemed to intimidate people. The typical dark jersey shirts he wore had a single pocket, large enough to fit his box of More Menthols. He smoked often, sometimes a pack a day. Daily, he also drank several cans of Coors, Michelob, or any other beer that was on sale. He seemed to be on edge often, as he chewed his index finger or scratched his hairy arms. Other times, his mind would drift far away. I wished I knew what he was thinking.

Time had not spared me either. I no longer looked like the woman Rio had left in Cuba. My black hair had turned white, but the girls had convinced me to bleach it, and with my pinkish skin, I might have looked more German than Cuban, except that—at the risk of stereotyping—my short height betrayed me. I was in great shape for Cuban standards, but not for my new adoptive country, where much thinner women were in style. Still, my looks were the last thing I cared about. So much more occupied my mind: my children's future, the sister I had left in Cuba, my new life with Rio, and especially the strange way he behaved.

If any man visited our Miami apartment, he would order the children to go into their bedroom and remain there until the visitor left.

"Why do the children need to hide?" I asked him, but he embraced me with the same warmth he did years before when we were newlyweds. He kissed me on the lips and asked me not to worry. Each time he kissed me that way, I remembered why I had fallen in love with him. I pictured him sitting behind his desk at the window factory in Havana, leaning back, the smell of his musky cologne weakening my legs and those of the other women at the factory.

My mother warned me not to marry him. She told me I should marry a lawyer or an attorney, but I knew he was the one from the moment I saw him.

I decided to give Rio some space and stopped asking questions for a while, but as time passed, it became clear there was much about my husband I did not know.

I owed Rio our freedom—one that had come at a price. When Rio went to Havana to claim us, he had included my sister and her family on his request, but later, after the government officials arrived at our house on Zapote Street to take us to the Port of Mariel, we learned that their list did not include them. I'd had no choice but to leave my sister and her family behind.

And here we were, during the summer of 1980, Rio and I together again after twelve years apart, acting and feeling like newlyweds, but with two teenage daughters, Tania and Lynette, and Gustavo, our eleven-year-old boy.

Chapter 2 – The Beginning

I didn't know Rio the way most wives know their husbands after being married over sixteen years. Our separation, imposed upon our family by the Cuban government, had impacted us in different ways than a divorce. Divorces have a more definitive outcome. In our case, our lives had remained in a stage of suspended animation, where the government held all the cards. Time had changed us, and we were about to discover just how much.

I enjoyed seeing the kids talking to their father about school, and acting around him as if he had always been in their lives. Gustavo, especially, glowed when he spent time with his father. I watched the two interact, noticing their resemblance, from their thin bodies and handsome faces, to their sense of humor.

For years, the children in the neighborhood had told Gustavo he did not have a father, and now, he could not spend enough time with Rio.

"Come on, Dad. Let me help you clean the car," he would tell him. Rio would smile and look at me with thankful eyes.

The family Rio had dreamed during the years of his childhood in an orphanage was at last complete, but his adult past insisted on pursuing him.

One hot and humid afternoon, Rio treated the children and me to ice cream. We walked on Miami's 8th Street, or *Calle Ocho*, as the locals call it, dressed in casual summer shorts, t-shirts, and sandals. Rio smelled like Pierre Cardin cologne, his favorite. Our children examined their surroundings in awe, watching the well-dressed people on their way to a theater as the aroma of fried food from a nearby cafeteria captivated our senses.

"What's that smell?" Gustavo asked, wide-eyed.

"It smells like *croquetas*," said Rio.

Gustavo turned to me and raised his eyebrows, but I shook my head, and he shrugged.

I had taught my children not to ask for things and to be grateful. When we lived in Cuba, for years, I'd had three jobs and worked twelve hours a day. That was what it took to dress my three children and put food on the table. Their father, being an immigrant in the United States with no formal education, had not been able to help me much. This thrifty existence had taught my children to understand the concept of sacrifice and the value of things, perhaps more so than others who had both parents.

Rio looked around him with a concerned expression, watching with suspicion the people who passed by. After a while, his eyes remained focused across the street. When I looked in the same direction, I noticed a man watching us, not casually, but as if he wanted us to notice him. The man was in his mid-thirties, muscular, with black hair and a mustache, jeans, and a black shirt.

"Girls, Gustavo, stop!" ordered Rio, and then he whispered in my ear: "Wait for me here and watch the kids. That guy across the street has been following us."

I tried to persuade him not to do anything, but he ignored me and yelled at the man: "Hey, you! What are you looking at?"

The stranger glanced at him calmly, shook his head and laughed. Rio did not take his eyes off of him. Instead, he raised his head slightly and closed his fists while his face contorted in anger.

"You think I'm funny?" Rio yelled, but the man continued to stare and smiled with sarcasm.

I noticed a well-dressed, elderly woman and her husband inconspicuously glancing at Rio with disapproval. She whispered something to her husband after they passed by. I felt embarrassed. I grabbed Rio by his arm, but he freed himself from my grasp and asked me to leave him alone.

Chapter 2 – The Beginning

"You want me to wipe that grin off your face, you motherfucker?" Rio asked the man who seemed unaffected by my husband's threat.

"Rio, watch the language!" I whispered. Rio did not respond. He grabbed a brown leather bag he carried under his arm, opened its zipper, and reached in. He then turned to me and said, "Stay here with the children. I'll be back."

"Please, let's keep walking. He's only looking. I don't want any problems," I said.

But my husband turned his back to me and walked away. He could not cross the street right away—it was packed with cars passing in both directions, some with the headlights on, now that the sun was going down. When he finally crossed, the man stayed where he was, seemingly unafraid. My eyes remained fixed on my husband. I saw him exchange some words with the stranger.

For a moment, a truck obstructed my view, and when it finally moved, I noticed the gun in Rio's hands. "*What is he doing?*" I asked myself. I swallowed and felt a knot in my stomach. The man began to walk away, looking back a couple of times and laughing. I didn't understand what was going on.

Were my children at risk? Did I need to start worrying about my family's safety? I knew Rio had a past. He had been alone in a big country, away from everyone he loved, and trouble had found him. He promised me that he had left that life behind. But had he? Was this man who was following us now connected in some way to Rio's past?

After Rio saw the man disappear in the distance, he crossed the street and rejoined us.

"Is everything okay, Dad?" Tania asked.

"Yes. Don't worry," he said, patting her on her back and smiling like nothing had happened. "Well, what flavor of ice cream do you all want?"

"Vanilla," said Gustavo, his eyes sparkling, a smile adorning his face.

"Chocolate for me," said Tania, shoving her long, light brown hair to one side with an air of self-importance.

"And me, strawberry," added Lynette, the only one of our children who had inherited the Chinese features of her paternal great-grandmother: long, straight, dark hair and slightly slanted, beautiful dark eyes.

Rio smiled and caressed Lynette's hair. "It figures!" he said, not surprised that each of our children wanted a different flavor of ice cream.

Later, as we sat on silver metal chairs at a round table in a semi-crowded ice cream parlor on *Calle Ocho*, we devoured our ice cream with pleasure and talked about silly things—all along, my mind wandering, my eyes trying to read Rio's, his attempting to reassure me.

That evening, our telephone rang around midnight. I saw Rio rise and pick up the handset from the nightstand.

"Hello . . . hello." No answer.

Rio angrily slammed the telephone down. An hour later, another ring, and, again, no one on the other end. He disconnected the telephone for the rest of the night. At first, he did not want to talk about it, but when the calls continued the next day, he told me he was going out for cigarettes.

He was gone for some time, while his mother and I prepared lunch for the family: black beans, rice, fried eggs, and plantains. By the time he returned, he found me in the kitchen slicing plantains. He walked behind me, placed his arms around me and kissed me on the cheek.

"Can we talk?" he asked.

I followed him quietly to our bedroom. After he closed the door, we both sat on the bed next to each other.

"I have booked a red-eye to Tampa for you, Mom, and the girls," he whispered. "You're leaving Miami tomorrow night. Gustavo and I will take as much as we can in the car."

"Leaving Miami? Can you please tell me what is going on?"

"It's not safe here," he said.

"But, Rio. You promised that you were no longer . . ."

"I'm not," he said. "You don't understand."

"Understand what?" I said, and looked into hazel eyes, trying to read what was in his mind.

"It is not that easy to walk away from my past. If we stay here, I will end up in a body bag. Please don't ask any more questions. The less you know, the safer you and the children will be."

"You were only a bodyguard, and your boss is dead now. That is what you told me. Who's after you?" I asked.

"This conversation is over, Laura."

I didn't insist. After all, I knew nothing about this new country. I was like a child learning to take her first steps. It was settled.

We talked to the rest of our family that evening. The children asked a lot of questions, but seemed excited about the idea of a new city, especially Tania. She did not like the school in Miami. She noticed that her classmates stayed away from the immigrant kids. She was a smart girl who had always performed well at school, yet here she found herself sitting in class, unable to understand what the teachers were saying and with no one to help her.

I felt guilty. I'd forced her to leave everything she knew behind to come to a new country.

I knew nothing about Tampa, Florida. Rio had been in New York, New Orleans, New Jersey, and Miami, but never in Tampa. He could not tell me much about it, except that it was a quiet, family-friendly city; smaller and much less intimidating than Miami.

During the brief time we lived in Miami, we experienced two very different cities: one with a beautiful downtown filled with the tallest buildings I had ever seen, and another immersed in chaos. In May 1980, the people in Liberty City rioted on the streets and burned cars and buildings, in response to the acquittal of police officers involved in the death of a man. It was the only time I saw Rio run a red light on purpose.

For years, I had lived in a country where its citizens could not protest against the government, even peacefully. Acts of civil unrest—like those I witnessed in Liberty City—would have been unimaginable.

While we lived in Miami, I shopped at a Sedano's supermarket almost every week. The full shelves brought tears to my eyes. So much food surrounded us and, unlike in Cuba, where rice, beans, potatoes, and meats, if available, were restricted to a meager quota, in Miami, I did not need a ration card to purchase anything. I remember telling my children, "You see? This is the country I wanted to show you all these years. Here, if you work and study hard, the possibilities are endless."

The children, my mother-in-law, Mayda, and I each gained several pounds during our time in Miami. Sometimes, the large meals made me nauseated. They also made me think about my sister and her family. She would have given her right arm to be able to purchase food for her daughters from supermarkets like the ones in Miami.

As I sat on the airplane that would take us to Tampa, I watched my daughters' curious faces looking around them. Tania did not touch anything, but Lynette pushed every button. At one point, the attendant came over to see what Lynette wanted. I did not understand what she asked us, but I shook my head and gave her an apologetic look. She nodded, forced a smile and walked away. This was the children's first time inside an airplane.

So many first experiences were overloading my senses. Nothing seemed real. After we struggled to buckle our seatbelts, I wondered how our life in Tampa would be. Would I have to worry about Rio's past following him everywhere we went? Would the United States become the place of dreams I had told my children about when they were growing up, or would it become our worst nightmare?

Chapter 3 - Tampa

Tania, Lynette, Mayda, and I did not know where to go when we disembarked the airplane upon our arrival at Tampa International Airport.

"Let's follow the other passengers," I said.

It was late, probably past midnight by the time we arrived, and all the stores and restaurants along our path were closed. After a short walk, we rode a monorail that took us to an area where a group of people waited for arriving passengers. We looked around and noticed a middle-aged blonde woman and a man with salt-and-pepper hair holding a sign that I could not read from where I was. The woman waved at us.

"Nelia and Tom?" I asked.

They smiled and nodded. Nelia rushed to me and gave me a warm hug, as if she had known me all my life. Then she embraced Mayda and the girls.

"Look how pretty your daughters are," she said. "Rio has told me so much about all of you."

"Welcome to Tampa," her husband said, shaking my hand and Mayda's.

"Thank you for meeting us this late," I said. "I did not mean to bother you."

"It's no bother at all," Tom said. "Rio is a good friend."

I looked around us and noticed that the passengers we were following had disappeared.

"I have no idea where to go next," I said.

"Don't worry," Nelia said. "Let's take the escalator down to luggage claim."

While we went down, a big sign on a wall above the escalator reading "Welcome to Tampa" made me smile.

It was not difficult to find where to go after we descended. Our flight was the only one that had landed at that time, and the passengers gathered by one of the carousels and waited. I recognized some of the people in the group I was following earlier.

Later, when the conveyor belt started to move, I had difficulty finding our luggage. On one occasion, I took one thinking it was mine, but another passenger approached me, mumbled something I did not understand, and grabbed it from me.

Once we managed to collect our luggage, we took the elevator to the short-term parking lot. It was warm and humid outside, but the cold air-conditioner in Tom's car in no time made me wish I had brought a sweater.

Later, as we drove away from the airport towards the Town and Country neighborhood, I noticed the light traffic—much lighter than in Miami.

"Where are the people?" I asked Nelia.

She started to laugh.

"Sleeping," she said. "I know what you are thinking, but Tampa is very different than Havana and even Miami. You will not see too many people walking on the sidewalks. Most people have cars. A car in Tampa is a necessity."

"I heard Rio say that before," I said.

I glanced at the closed stores and gas stations along the way. The streets and buildings looked clean and orderly, but I did not see many palm trees, like in Cuba and Miami. Instead, oak trees dotted the landscape.

My daughters looked outside, curious about their surroundings.

"This will be our home, girls," I told Tania and Lynette.

Mayda's eyes wandered outside the window. She said little along the way.

"It is a nice place to live," Nelia said. "We like it very much."

As we approached the area of Town and Country, I noticed fewer businesses and more residential areas. We turned onto one of the residential streets and, after driving for a little while, Tom stopped in front of one of the duplexes.

"We are here!" he announced.

"It's not very far from the airport."

"No, it's not," said Nelia, reaching into her purse. "Let me give you the key and help you get settled. You will find used mattresses and sheets in the bedrooms, toilet paper, soap, a few towels, and cups, but the house is not furnished. It does have a bar with a few bar stools in the kitchen."

"Thank you," I said. "I was prepared to sleep on the floor tonight. You have done more than enough. I will pay you back as soon as we begin to work."

"Laura, we do not expect anything from you," Nelia said. "If we do not help our fellow men in their moment of need, what does that make us?"

I shook my head. "You are an angel," I said.

Tom brought our luggage in and inspected every room.

"You can never be too safe," he said. "Make sure you lock the door when we leave."

His comment made me nervous at first, but moments later I told myself that Tom was being over-protective.

Before they left, Nelia hugged us again and her husband waved good-bye.

"Tell Rio I will stop by tomorrow," he said. "He should be here by then."

After Nelia and Tom drove away, the girls went through every room.

"It's a big place," said Tania. "We won't have to sleep in the living room anymore."

"Let's go to bed," I said. "Tomorrow is a busy day. Your father will be arriving in a few hours."

Rio and Gustavo arrived the next day, and by the following Monday, Rio started to work at a 7-Eleven convenience store. I found a job cleaning rooms at a motel off Dale Mabry Highway, near the Tampa Stadium–or the Big Sombrero, as I heard Rio call it.

"This stadium is the home of the Tampa Bay Buccaneers, a football team," he told me when we passed by it the first time.

I did not know anything about football, and we could not afford to go to the stadium, but sometimes, when games were televised, Rio would tell me how it was played. It energized me to see the people of Tampa dressed up in orange colors when the Bucs played in town. Football brought them together and gave families of various backgrounds one common purpose: to see their team win.

Each night, after dinner, I began to relearn English. I had been an English tutor in Cuba, but had lost my ability to speak the language after not using it for so many years. My accent was thick, and I had to keep repeating myself because people would look at me, completely clueless, when I spoke. After a while, I decided not to tell anyone else about my tutoring days.

To help our family, Rio's boss allowed him to bring leftovers home. The kids enjoyed these meals: burritos, tacos, and other fast food they had not eaten before.

But it did not take us long to realize that the house in Town and Country was too expensive. Electricity, water, gasoline, and rent consumed most of our checks.

One Sunday morning, while I reviewed the classified section on the *Tampa Tribune* newspaper, I found an old frame house in a working class neighborhood known as West Tampa that was for sale by the owner. Rio and I went to see it. It needed paint and new wood floors. It had three bedrooms, one bathroom, and an overgrown backyard guarded by a chain-link fence. It was close to I-275 and downtown, and the neighborhood seemed eerily quiet.

"Are you sure we can afford to buy a house?" Rio asked me.

"Yes. I borrowed my boss's calculator to estimate the principal and interest payments. My boss told me to factor insurance, taxes, and estimated repairs, and gave me an idea of what to expect. It's all there. It is better to buy than to rent."

I handed Rio a piece of paper with some calculations, and he looked at it.

"Will we save that much?" he asked.

I nodded. He took a deep breath.

"Well, let's buy ourselves a house," he said.

It took a while to convince the owner to give us credit, but I could not contain my happiness when he did.

The much cheaper house allowed us to purchase used bedroom furniture and to save some of our money. I wanted to save more, but Rio would not limit his credit-card purchases.

Between his cigarettes, his beer, and his insistence on surprising the kids with special meals—from three-cheese pizzas with pepperoni and ham to different types of lasagnas—we could not bring down our credit-card balances.

I realized that, if we wanted our family to get ahead, one of us had to take control of our finances. Without telling him, I began to put money away. I hid it inside an envelope in a briefcase where I kept the important papers.

When I had enough money saved, I hid it with our check deposits and sent larger payments to our landlord. I became obsessed with reducing our debt. I also tried to persuade Rio to spend less on credit cards.

"If we keep paying interest on these cards, we will never get our head above water," I protested.

He looked at me and rolled his eyes.

"You always want to ruin all the fun," he said. "I want my kids to have a good life."

"They will if we stop throwing money away," I said.

It was an endless battle.

At the end of the summer, we signed the children up for school. The girls had been in different grades in Cuba, but we wanted them to be together, so we registered both of them to begin the tenth grade at Jefferson High School.

My two youngest children seemed to adapt well, but Tania often kept to herself, spending hours either studying or writing. Sometimes, she asked her father or me to assist her with school assignments. Rio could not help her. His training at the orphanage he'd attended until he was seventeen had focused on the inner workings of machines.

"I can help you with math, my love," I would tell her. "I will not be much help with the other subjects. My English is not strong enough."

In Cuba, she'd had excellent grades, but in the United States, her inability to understand her teachers was affecting her qualifications, no matter how many hours she spent translating her homework to Spanish. Occasionally, she would yell and throw her notebook across the room in frustration.

One Sunday, I was on my way to the restroom when I heard the door of her bedroom open.

"What are you doing up? It's only four," I said.

"I have a headache. I can't sleep."

"Do you want to talk about what's bothering you?"

She shook her head and looked down.

"Your father has a bottle of a pill called Tylenol that is supposed to work well. Take one. We are not used to it, but it is better than nothing. Do you want one?"

"No, thanks. I just need to be alone," she said.

I kissed her forehead and returned to my room. Three hours later, when I woke up, I found her sitting on the sofa, her legs crossed.

"Did you sleep?" I asked her.

"I wasn't sleepy," she said.

"Do you want to talk about what's bothering you?"

Once again, she shook her head and looked away.

I left her in the living room and went to the girls' bedroom to talk to Lynette. She was just waking up when I walked in.

"Do you know what's wrong with your sister?" I asked her.

Lynette yawned and rubbed her eyes.

"She is mad about her grades, but she also misses her boyfriend, Uncle Antonio and Aunt Berta," she said.

Lynette's words took me back to the night we left our house in Havana.

Tania had said good-bye to her boyfriend the night before. A few hours later, in the middle of the night, a white government car parked by the curb in front of our house. I was asleep when I heard the knocks on the door. When I opened it, two officials came into the living without being invited, then ordered us to get dressed and to not take anything out of the house. Our clothes, our shoes, my university diplomas, the family pictures, the letters Rio had sent me during the years we spent apart, and everything else we owned had to stay behind.

We dressed quickly and said good-bye to my sister and her husband—their daughters were still asleep. I was giving my sister one last embrace, when an officer ordered us to go outside with him. My children looked frightened and confused.

"Let's go, kids," I said. I grabbed Gustavo by the hand and walked out to the porch, followed by the girls. My sister stood on the front porch to watch us leave.

We crammed into the back seat of the Russian-made car. Moments later, as it sped away, our eyes focused on the dark, quiet streets, the unpainted colonial-style houses, the broken sidewalks, and the corner *bodega* where we had often stood in line for hours to buy our assigned quotas of rice, beans, eggs, and—if we got lucky—a few ounces of beef, pork, or chicken.

"Where are you taking us?" I asked.

No answer.

I looked at my children. Tania sat between the window and me and tried to conceal her emotions, but her erratic breathing, her quivering lips, and the sliding of her index fingers beneath her eyes gave her away. Lynette and Gustavo glanced at me and shrugged.

The two officials stopped a couple of times to consult a piece of paper they carried, probably an address, and after a while, I noticed we were approaching the municipality of Marianao, where my mother-in-law lived. The car parked in front of Mayda's tiny corner house shortly after.

Mayda had not known the officers would be coming for us that night. Otherwise, she would have given all the money she had hidden in jars to her sister. Most of it would have to stay behind, except some she had concealed from the officers and given to her sister when she hugged her good-bye.

Once Mayda joined us, I placed Gustavo on my lap, and my mother-in-law asked Tania to sit on hers, as Tania weighed less than her sister. Despite my best efforts to make Tania eat, her poor appetite and refusal to eat had made her bony and undernourished.

We left the municipality of Marianao and continued our drive through the quiet streets and avenues of Havana. Few people roamed the streets at that hour, and most of the ones we saw looked young, probably returning home after attending house parties.

"Do you know where they are taking us?" Mayda whispered.

"No," I said. "They are not answering any questions."

The officers stopped in front of the Abreu Fontán building in Miramar, a structure that had been used as a social club, but that, we later learned, was being utilized as a processing center. When we entered, I noticed it was packed with families.

My children, my mother-in-law, and I sat on plastic chairs in a large waiting room, and Gustavo immediately began to ask questions about his father. While I answered him, I saw Tania sobbing quietly. I shook my head and began to scan my surroundings, afraid that her crying would not lead to anything good.

It had not taken long for me to realize what was happening: if government officials caught children crying, they took them to a separate room, and I never saw the children return to their families again.

I was about to speak to Tania about it, when a doctor who was probably in his mid-forties approached me quietly and asked the children and me to follow him. He led us through a narrow, scarcely lit hallway to his office, closed the door, and proceeded to explain what was going on, which confirmed my suspicion.

"My children and I had been kept away from my husband for almost twelve years," I explained. "Please help me."

He bit his finger and looked at me nervously.

"I will," he said, and took a deep breath.

He proceeded to open his drawer and gave Tania a pill.

"What is this?" she asked.

"It will calm you down," he said.

She crossed her arms.

"No, I refuse to take anything! Those pills only fry the brain."

"I agree that abusing them is not good, but in your case, it can save your life," said the doctor.

"What do you mean?" she asked.

"Tania, no more arguments. Do what the doctor says this very second," I said.

She finally did.

Before I left the office, on the doctor's desk, I noticed a black-and-white picture of the doctor, his beautiful wife, and their three children. I looked at him, smiled, and thanked him.

Later, as I huddled my children around me, I told them:

"This is the day that you become men and women. No more crying. I have waited a long time to leave this place, and you will not, you cannot destroy the only opportunity we have to leave. Your future is in your hands."

I did not see them cry again. Despite being only fifteen, thirteen, and eleven then, they became adults that day.

Rumors in Havana spread quickly, and when Tania's boyfriend learned what had happened, he rushed to our house, where he found that my sister, Berta, was about to leave to bring me some papers I needed. He asked my sister to take him to see Tania.

Seeing the young man's desperation and not knowing what was happening at the processing center, she allowed him to accompany her. When Berta told me he was outside, I asked her to make up a story and tell him that Tania would write to him when she reached the United States.

I had no intentions of ever telling her. He was her first love. Why make her suffer anymore? He would never hear from her again.

I did not see Tania cry again until we arrived in the United States. Part of me believed that she blamed me for the long separation from her father, and now, for the loss of everything she had. I felt that no matter what I did, she would never trust me.

A few months after we moved to LaSalle Street, I saw Tania talking to a tall, large-boned blond boy who lived in our neighborhood. They were teaching each other the names of various objects in their respective languages.

"Why didn't you invite him in?" I asked her.

She shook her head.

"Our house doesn't have nice furniture. I don't want him to see how we live."

I could not help her feel better about living in our scarcely-furnished home, but I appreciated her honesty. Lynette later told me that Tania only liked this boy as a friend, but I was happy to see that she had taken the first step in leaving her previous life behind.

Our move to Tampa marked the start of a new chapter. There, our lives would change in ways I would have never dreamed of. I was ready for a new start.

Chapter 4 - My Sister's Letter

Rio and I arrived from work that evening and found a letter from my sister on the kitchen counter. I missed her. She had been the voice of reason in my life while I lived in Cuba, my center, and the person who grounded me. Not realizing that sometimes I had to live "in the clouds" to make sense of our nonsensical surroundings, she used to tell me "stop dreaming so much." But dreaming had kept me going.

The house was noisy as usual. Tania was doing her homework and protesting about not understanding the instructions. Lynette and Gustavo listened to music in the living room and laughed at a story Lynette was telling her brother. Their grandmother sat on a chair near them, lost in thought.

I dropped off my purse on the kitchen counter and went to my bedroom to read my sister's letter privately. I noticed that the white envelope still appeared to be sealed. I felt relieved. Some said that government officials would read letters sent to the exterior. The number of pages told me something was not right, as she tended to be concrete and to the point. Worried, I sat on my bed and began to read. The letter was dated June 25, 1980. "Dear Laura," it began:

About a month ago, government officials came to pick us up early in the morning. They told us that a boat awaited at the Port of Mariel to take us to the United States and that we were leaving that evening. You can imagine my excitement when they came. We were not allowed to take anything, but I gave away all of our food to the neighbors. With all the necessity and hunger, I did not want it to go to waste. You know me, always worried about everyone.

I was happy and nervous at the same time. Something kept telling me that it had been too easy.

That afternoon, while we were at the processing center, after several long hours without eating, my fears materialized, when one of the officers reviewed our papers and he told me: "You and the girls can leave, but your husband has to stay." I saw your entire life in fast-forward when he pronounced these words, and my world crumbled. I did not want to repeat your mistake. As much as I wanted to see you and the kids and to give my daughters the chance at a decent life, I could not do it at the expense of their father. I knew what being alone could do to him. He would not have survived it.

I was disappointed and angry. I had already handed the keys to my house to the woman from the CDR. I wondered where would we go. What would we do? I did not understand why this was happening. Later, someone told me that he could not leave because he was an engineer.

I told the officer: "If my husband cannot leave, I will not leave either."

We exited the processing center feeling like deflated beach balls. We were starving. We stopped a cab and explained our situation to the driver. The young man was very nice and understanding and took us home at no charge, but when I arrived, I had no key.

I went to see Carmen, from the CDR. Luckily, she still had the keys and returned them to me. But we had no food in the house as I had given it all away. That evening, we ate a piece of hard bread. The girls, especially my youngest, were crying. She is only eight. She did not understand what was going on.

And you know the irony of all this? After the government would not allow Antonio to leave because he is an engineer, he was not allowed to work in that capacity.

I used all the money I had hidden in the house to buy guavas and sugar in the black market. Antonio goes to Párraga, where his parents used to live, and buys them there. He helps me peel them, and we cook all day. Actually, he cannot help me as much anymore. When the government realized he had been out of a "real" job for several weeks, he was told to either find a job or go to jail. They gave him a position at the park picking up garbage and cutting weeds with a machete. He is too weak for a job like that. As you know, he has spent his entire life buried in his books. His skin is so light, and the long hours in the sun are making him sick. He has lost a lot of weight. Probably his depression.

The girls see him carrying a machete on his way to work and tell their friends that he is a machetero.

Now, I don't know how long we will be apart. But I want you to know that I understand you better than I ever did. I'm sorry for not realizing the hell you were in when you and Rio were kept apart.

Things are getting bad for those of us who stayed behind and want to leave. We fear for our lives, but I have to remain hopeful.

My marriage has strengthened as a result of all this. Antonio now understands how important he is to me. You know I am not one for sentimentalities, and often, he has wondered if I loved him.

I know I have told you more than I should have. I do not want you to worry. I will find a way. You know I always do.

I miss you and the kids very much and hope to see you again one day. Say hello to them on my behalf. They need to understand the sacrifice you made for their futures. Tell them to study hard and to make you proud. I have high hopes for them.

Love,

Berta.

After I finished reading, I stared blankly at the letter, and feelings of emptiness and uselessness overwhelmed me. I was still sitting on the edge of the bed when Rio walked in.

"Is everything ok?"

I shook my head.

"What happened?"

I gave him Berta's letter and he read quietly. I noticed him taking deep breaths occasionally while he read. When he was done, his eyes were moist. He shook his head and returned the letter to me.

"Sons of bitches!" he said closing his fists and storming out of the room.

My husband loved Berta like a sister. From the moment Rio and I met, they had made a connection. When my mother opposed my marriage to Rio, my sister had played the role of intermediary to help her understand that she should not interfere.

My mother had wanted me to marry a refined, educated man, but I had fallen in love with someone without a college education, whom she considered wild and unpredictable.

Prior to the revolution, Rio had worked as an industrial mechanic. Castro's revolution triumphed on January 1, 1959, and a couple of years later, Rio and I met. By then, he was working as a manager for a glass company and became my boss. I fell in love with him the moment I saw him, but I kept my feelings secret, as he was engaged. Rio was flirtatious. He loved women and women loved him. I was his friend and confidant for a long time, advising him on what gifts to buy for his girlfriend and listening to him when he spoke about other women. It was clear to me that I was not the type of woman he would go after.

Eventually, when Rio discovered that his fiancée could not give him a family, despite his love for her, he left her. That same day, upset and not thinking clearly, Rio rode his motorcycle fast through El Malecón, Havana's waterfront, and lost control of it. For days, Rio struggled between life and death. When he awoke and found me by his side, he began to understand just how much I loved him. It did not take long for him to ask me to be his wife.

Rio had been trained as an expert shooter, loved to have fun, and had slept with many women before we started to date. These were not the qualities my mother wanted in my future husband, but my sister did not judge him. Rio appreciated that she had accepted him the way he was, and they became like brother and sister.

I folded Berta's letter and left my room to look for Rio. I found him in the backyard, under the oak tree, smoking a cigarette. I embraced him and kissed his cheeks. I felt the moisture of his tears against my lips.

Chapter 5 - My Grandmother

"Come on, girls," my mother said, when she opened the door to the bedroom I shared with my sister. "Get up! Time to go to school. You need to learn as much as you can today, so you don't have to work as hard as your father and I do."

She said that often, not with resentment, but with the conviction that we would have a better life than she and my father had.

My mother adapted quickly to the United States, even faster than my father. She had spent years talking about the amazing life that awaited us, and now, she was ready to do everything in her power to ensure we took advantage of the opportunities our new life afforded us.

Her university education, with a concentration in law and mathematics, gave her an edge over my father, and made it easy for her to convince him that we would never get ahead unless we bought a house and stopped renting.

On the day they closed on our LaSalle house, when we opened the door, my parents acted like newlyweds. I had only seen them that happy when Castro initiated the *viajes de la comunidad* and my father was able to visit us in Cuba, ten years after his departure. They hugged each other and kissed in front of us, despite my mother's protest that my father should not get that affectionate in front of the children. My grandmother, on the other hand, followed my father around the house with an empty expression. Since her fainting incident at the camp, she had not been the same, and the situation only worsened with the passage of time.

During the day, my siblings and I went to school, my parents carpooled to their jobs, and my grandmother stayed alone. She was not particularly fond of television, and I never saw her reading a book. When she lived in Cuba, she lived off the money she saved prior to the revolution, money she took out of the bank and hid in jars. She also tended to her garden, but in Tampa, we did not have a garden, only ugly shrubs that had seen better days. After she cooked dinner for the family, she had little to do.

"I have written several letters to Ricardo, but he is not answering them," she told me one day. Ricardo was her second husband. Mom said he was not our grandfather, and she did not allow us to call him Grandpa or to be affectionate with him. "I think he's dead," my grandmother added as she looked down and played with her arthritic fingers.

I caressed her wavy white hair and gave her a kiss.

"Don't say that, Grandma. Maybe, he has not received your letters. You know how long it takes for them to get there. More than a month! That, or maybe they were never delivered. Mail delivery in Cuba is not very reliable."

But no one could convince her that he was fine.

My mother used to tell us that when two people loved each other with all their heart, it did not matter how far apart they were. Their love for each other created a bond that distance could not destroy.

"Remember the day your maternal grandmother died in Cuba, and your father called me from the United States because he felt something was wrong?" Mom would tell us. She was convinced that my father had felt her pain. That led me to believe that there could be truth in my grandmother's assertions regarding her husband.

My grandmother and I sat by a white dining-room table that one of our neighbors had given us three months after we moved to LaSalle Street. She was writing a letter to her sister, while I worked diligently on my homework. In the living room, my brother and sister listened to a Bee Gees' record, another gift from one of our neighbors, while my sister tried to sing along to "How Deep is Your Love." Gustavo kept asking her to be quiet and let him enjoy the music, but the more he begged, the louder she sang, making up half the words. She did not understand their meaning or how to pronounce them.

Suddenly, the front door opened and my parents came in, each holding two bags of groceries in their arms. Grandma quickly got up and offered to serve them dinner.

"No, thank you, Mom," my father said. "It was a long day at work. We will shower first and serve ourselves later. How was your day?"

She shrugged.

"I tried to speak to a neighbor today," she said, "but I could not understand her. It's frustrating when you cannot even talk to a neighbor and have to spend hours looking at these four walls . . . Anyways, don't worry about it."

Grandma shook her head, but my father seemed too preoccupied to pay attention to what she had said.

"Did anyone call?" Dad asked.

Ever since my father had activated his new telephone number, he seemed obsessed about knowing every detail about our callers. He even questioned salespeople, like a detective in an interrogation room.

"The telephone rang once, but by the time I answered it, I did not hear anyone on the other side," said my grandmother. "Maybe they hung up."

Chapter 5 - My Grandmother

My father's face contorted with a worried look, as he and my mother exchanged glances. Moments later, he took a deep breath and followed Mom to their bedroom.

"Why is your father so worried about who calls?" Grandma asked.

I shrugged.

"Don't worry about it," I said. "You know Dad. He worries too much. That's why he has hardly any hair left on his head."

She smiled and shook her head.

"Let's go to the backyard to talk about Cuba," I said. "I'm done with my homework, and I like to listen to your stories."

That was one of the few things my grandmother enjoyed: talking to me about Cuba. Half the time, she repeated the same stories, over and over again, but I would make believe I had not heard them before. She told me about her eleven brothers and sisters, most of them dead now. She spoke about the son she had lost and the residential real-estate rental business she built after her first husband died. The government had taken her houses after the revolution, leaving her with only one.

As we sat under the oak tree, a mild breeze played with my hair. I tucked it behind my ear, while my grandmother combed it gently. When she was done, I turned around and hugged her. She smiled and caressed my face.

The sun had set on the horizon, and a floodlight, in the rear of the house, illuminated us. The sweet and smoky aroma of barbecued beef from a nearby house made my stomach growl, but my grandmother did not seem to notice it.

"You and your sister look so different," she said, while she took my hand and placed it between hers. "Your sister, with her straight, long hair and slanted eyes from my Chinese great-grandmother, and you with your honey-colored eyes, fair skin, and light-brown hair from your mother's European ancestors. Your brother is a mixture of his parents, but of all my grandchildren, I think that you are the only one who cares about me."

"You know that's not true," I said. "We all love you."

"You don't understand," she said. "How could you? You are too young. When people are old, like me, they get in the way. I should've never left Cuba. Why? To come here and be a burden to everyone?"

"Everyone is busy, Grandma, but no one thinks you are a burden."

"Your brother and sister don't talk to me much," she said.

"They are younger than me, but they do love you." I said unsure of why she felt that way.

I devoted more time to her than my siblings because I felt we had a special bond. We understood each other. My mother had told me that when my father was nine, Grandma had lost a child and her first husband within months of each other. She'd placed my father in an orphanage after that, and Dad never forgave her. Grandma had thought that my father needed structure she could not provide. She'd done what she thought was best for him, but he never understood her or tried to get close to her, no matter how many gifts she bought for him with the small fortune she built after her husband passed away.

My grandmother deserved my love and devotion not only for being my grandmother, but she had always been one of the most loving and generous people I knew. Over the twelve years that my parents were apart, she had supplemented my mother's income by sending her one hundred pesos per month. This amount represented one person's salary in the Cuba of those years. In addition, every weekend, Grandma cooked us yellow rice and chicken, my favorite dish. I often wondered how, in a country where everything was rationed, she could do this. One day, I asked her.

"I trade the roses in my garden for chicken," she told me.

Plantain trees and other plants I did not recognize had surrounded her tiny one-bedroom house, in the Marianao neighborhood. As I walked around her backyard, which was surrounded with a concrete-block wall, it looked to me like a small forest. She had created this beautiful and serene environment with her own hands.

Grandma cooked her delicious yellow rice and chicken with beer to enhance the flavor, complementing it with the best fried plantains I had ever eaten, and when it was ready, she'd serve my siblings, Mom, and me first. She smiled when she witnessed our happiness as we ate each spoonful and celebrated her cooking, sometimes asking for second servings with our eyes. My mother would have punished us if we had asked any other way. Grandma always served us more.

"Why aren't you eating, Grandma?" I would ask her. Her answer was always the same. "I have already eaten."

But I did not think she was telling me the truth. After we were finished, she'd tell us:

"I will go wash the dishes. You stay here." She never allowed anyone to help her.

One day, disregarding her instructions, I waited a few minutes and went into the kitchen. I found her eating a small plate of yellow rice. At that moment, I understood. I never asked for second servings again.

Grandma took a deep breath and tucked her wavy white hair behind her ears. Her honey-colored eyes seemed lost somewhere beyond the leaves of the old oak tree.

"I miss Ricardo," she said. "I can only imagine how he felt when he came home the next morning, after work, and found an empty house. I was not able to say good-bye. I didn't know they were coming for us that night."

"Your sister lives next door and must have explained what happened. It was not your fault."

"But, I didn't even leave him a note."

"The officers were rushing you, Grandma. You had no time."

She shook her head.

"If he is alive, who will care for him now?"

"You can't think like that. He will be fine."

"You don't understand," she said. "When a man has been with a woman as long as we have, and is used to having her care for him, it is not easy when he suddenly finds himself alone."

I noticed a profound sadness in her gaze and not knowing what to do, I gave her a hug. She forced a smile.

"Don't worry about me," she said. "Anyhow, have you written anything today?"

I nodded.

"Early this morning, when everyone slept, I wrote a couple of poems."

"Do you want to read them to me?"

My eyes lit up. "Yes! Of course."

I ran inside and returned minutes later with my journal. I read the poems, and she listened attentively.

"You are a good writer," she told me after I was done. "One day, I want you to write a poem about how I feel."

"Whenever you are ready, just tell me exactly how you feel, and I will do my best to capture it in a poem," I answered.

A long time passed before she decided to tell me. By then, it was too late.

Grandma connected me to my roots and to Cuba in ways no one else could. I never shared my journals with anyone else in the house, but for some reason, I felt I could tell her anything.

Chapter 6 - First Halloween

Since our arrival to the United States, Rio would only allow the children to watch programs in the English language, insisting they had to train the ears. So often, I saw them watching reruns of a program called Star Trek that showed spaceship men and women dressed in tight, solid-colored outfits. In no time, I could hear Gustavo say, "Beam me up, Scottie."

Everything was strange in this new world, and there was still so much to learn, but more than anything, I wanted my children to succeed in America. Rio and I did not matter anymore; however, Tania, Lynette, and Gustavo had a chance. They had their entire lives ahead of them.

As part of our adaptation process, Rio suggested I stop calling Gustavo by his name and instead call him Gus.

"It will make him feel more at home," he said. "The name 'Gustavo' is too long. Americans will not be able to pronounce it."

I agreed to do so, but only in front of his friends.

As the granddaughter of Spanish immigrants who traveled to Cuba before I was born, I had learned early on the importance of blending into the culture and customs of the adoptive country. After all, I had no intention of ever returning to Cuba. This adaptation process affected what we watched on television and the food we ate. We no longer had a straight diet of beans and rice, but a full spectrum of new dishes we had never eaten before.

Sometimes, Rio cooked Chinese fried rice. Other times, he took us to McDonald's for a burger and an apple pie, or we enjoyed a barbecue in the backyard. Everyone in the family liked barbecued burgers except for Tania, who preferred hot dogs.

In Tampa, we also found many places that sold "Cuban sandwiches." I laughed the first time we bought one. Cuban sandwich? Rio said they had been invented in Ybor City, although people in Miami claimed they'd invented it. It consisted of "Cuban" bread, which did not resemble or taste like the bread we ate in Cuba, ham, Swiss cheese, roasted pork, pickles and mustard (although I preferred it with mayonnaise). I found the name of that sandwich amusing because Cubans had not seen ham and cheese for years.

We also had to get used to celebrating and eating turkey on Thanksgiving Day and exchanging gifts on Christmas. When we lived in Cuba, we'd hardly had enough money to eat, never mind to exchange gifts. One of the most interesting and intriguing traditions in the United States was Halloween. During our first one, Nelia invited us for dinner.

As we approached her house, around seven that October evening, I noticed a group of children dressed like ghosts, monsters, vampires, and wizards walking on the sidewalk and carrying either orange plastic pumpkins with black handles or large plastic bags. My husband parked our gray Chevette by the curb, and we had started to walk towards the front door, when the kids ran past us and rang the bell.

"Trick or treat!" they yelled, almost in unison, as Nelia's smiling face appeared behind the door. In her mid-forties, Nelia had a medium built, kind blue eyes, and wavy blond hair that reached her shoulders. She was wearing a floral blouse, black slacks and sandals.

She smiled, reached into a bag of candy, took a handful of wrapped pieces, and deposited a couple into the receptacle of each of the children.

"Thank you," some of them said, and ran towards the house across the street. A couple of them, a little older than the rest, did not say anything, examined what they had received, grimaced, and walked away.

Nelia's yard was decorated with a witch and a skeleton. A material that resembled spider webs blanketed her shrubs.

"Free candy?" Gustavo asked his father. I did not know what to answer, yet Rio was quick to respond.

"Yes, it's Halloween. Kids dress up and the neighbors give them candy."

"Why?" he asked.

"Tradition," said Rio.

Gustavo and Lynette looked at me with their eyes wide open. I shook my head.

Nelia greeted us warmly when she saw us and led us into her living room. As we entered, she hugged us and kissed our cheeks. Rio was the last one to enter and handed her a paper bag that contained a pumpkin pie he had purchased at a nearby Winn Dixie store. He had explained to me, on the way to Nelia's house, that it was customary to bring a dish when invited to dinner.

This was our first dinner invitation, and I felt uncomfortable. A few days before, when Rio had told me about it, I'd first refused to accept the invitation because there were too many of us, but I did not want Nelia to think I was ungrateful.

With a friendly demeanor, she asked us to sit down, placed the bag of candy on a table, and walked towards the rear of the house with the pie.

"Tom, they are here!" she yelled.

Rio and I sat on the floral loveseat and the kids on the matching sofa.

"Dad, can I go get candy like the other kids?" Gustavo asked, trying to avoid my eyes.

"Gustavo, what have I taught you?" I said firmly.

"You don't have an outfit," said Rio.

Our son looked down and began to play with his fingers. Lynette kept moving her legs, as she did when she was bored, and Tania looked around the room, her eyes focusing on a black-and-white picture of Nelia and her husband on their wedding day. We all stayed quiet for a moment. Then we heard footsteps approaching, and Nelia reappeared followed by her husband.

We all stood. Nelia's husband shook Rio's hand and mine. "Welcome, but please sit down," Tom said. "Well, I hope you came hungry. We cooked a lot of food. And where is your mom, Rio?"

"She wasn't feeling well," Rio said.

"She is very depressed because she misses her husband in Cuba," I added. "This trip has been very difficult for her."

"You mean, Rio's father?" Nelia asked, looking at Rio.

"No. My father passed away when I was a child."

"This is her second husband. But they are not actually married," I added. Rio glanced at me and raised his eyebrows. He was right. What was I thinking?

We heard more footsteps approaching from the back of the house, and moments later a boy and a girl appeared, the boy dressed like a monster and the girl in a princess outfit.

"We are going trick-or-treating, Mom!" said the thirteen-year old boy, as he walked towards the door, followed by his ten-year-old sister. Before they had a chance to reach the door, Nelia yelled. "Wait! Take Gustavo and the girls with you."

Gustavo glanced at his father, as if asking for permission.

"But Nelia, they don't have outfits," said Rio.

"They don't need them. Kids, help Gustavo paint his face. Girls, I have some plastic masks you can use."

"The girls are too old for trick-or-treating," said Rio.

"Too old? No one is too old for trick-or-treating. Come on, Rio. Don't spoil their first Halloween. I would go if I didn't have so much to do! Kids, come with me."

Gustavo sought his father's approval with his eyes.

"Go, go with Nelia," Rio said.

Lynette and Gustavo followed Nelia willingly, while Tania shrugged, glanced at me and raised her eyebrows. "Go with them," I said.

"I don't want candy," she said shyly.

"Come on. Go. This is a new experience for you. Don't be shy," I said.

Her cheeks turned a little pink, but moments later, she reluctantly stood and walked towards Nelia, looking back once with reproaching eyes. When we were alone, Rio whispered in my ear, "Why did you make her go?"

"She needs to get out of her shell," I said.

"I don't like my kids going to strangers' houses asking for candy," Rio said. "There are a lot of sick people out there."

"Nelia seems like a sensible woman. She would not send her own children out if it were not safe."

He shook his head, and we remained silent. I quietly looked at the decorations on the wall, the family pictures, a large floral painting above the sofa, the light green draperies that complemented the fabric on the sofa and the love seat.

"One day, I would love to have a house like this one. It is so pretty," I said.

Rio smiled. "We will, one day," he said. He placed his arm around me and squeezed me gently. "I love you," he whispered.

"Me too."

Chapter 6 - First Halloween

When Nelia and the children returned from the back of the house, they were ready; the boy with his face painted in white and black, and the girls with plastic monster masks. Each carried a plastic bag. Nelia's kids seemed even more excited than before now that they had company.

"Tania, make sure your brother behaves," said Rio.

"I will," said Tania.

After the children were gone, we talked with Nelia and her husband for a few minutes and then I followed her into the kitchen, while Rio and Tom stayed in the living room conversing.

"How can I help?" I asked.

"You don't need to do anything. Sit there," she said, pointing to a square wooden table with four chairs. "I will finish."

Nelia had a big kitchen with white cabinets, white Formica countertops, and a small window above the sink, adorned with a white-and-yellow curtain. Her kitchen was well organized. I loved her spice rack—my first time seeing one—and all the shiny kitchen utensils that she kept inside a decorative white ceramic holder.

"I feel bad that you are doing all this for us. The least I can do is to help you."

"Nonsense. Sit down and tell me, any news from your sister?"

"I received a letter from her," I said looking down at the impeccable beige tile floor that smelled like lemons. "Someone who visited Cuba delivered her letter. She didn't want to mail it, afraid that if the government opened it and discovered what she had written, she could become a bigger target than she already was."

Nelia shook her head before pouring the plantains into the hot oil.

"Are they okay?"

I took a deep breath.

"Not really. They both lost their jobs after we left."

"Oh my! How can they make a living with two kids? You had told me she was an architect and he an engineer. But why both of them? What happened?"

"After the Mariel boatlift, when thousands of people left Cuba, life became very difficult for those who wanted to leave," I said, touching the plastic table cover. "They became outcasts in their own country. Then, the acts of repudiation started."

"What do you mean?" said Nelia, turning her head towards me briefly.

"Trucks full of government supporters target the homes of those who want to leave. Many people have been taken out of their houses by force and beaten. One of those trucks came to our block, but Carmen, the woman in charge of the CDR, lied and said that there was no one in the neighborhood wishing to leave. She saved my sister and her family. We could never be able to repay her for what she has done."

"CDR?"

"I'm sorry. Committees of Defense of the Revolution."

"Isn't Carmen a socialist?" asked Nelia, her brow furrowed.

"She was at first, but she changed," I said. "She was the only person in our neighborhood who owned a telephone. For years, while Rio and I were apart, she allowed me to call him from her house. She didn't understand why my family was kept apart for so many years."

"Your family has been lucky to have her," she said. I nodded.

"I'm so sorry, Laura. What do they do to feed themselves?"

The oil splashed as Nelia turned the plantains in the big frying pan.

“She buys guavas and sugar in the black market and sells marmalade for two pesos a jar,” I said, as I pensively visualized my sister’s life in Cuba. I then remembered that the man from whom we used to purchase marmalade when we lived in Cuba had killed himself, so my sister did not have any competition.

“That is a tough way to make a living,” she said.

“It is,” I said. “She has to sell 150 jars to replace her income. Her husband could not find a job at first, but after the exodus, the garbage began to pile up on the streets, and there was no one to pick it up. He was able to secure a job picking up garbage for a little while. Then, he worked at a park. My brother-in-law has spent his life buried in books and is not used to physically-demanding jobs. He is very depressed.”

We remained silent for a while. Nelia turned off the stove and began to remove the plantains from the hot oil.

“Any chance they will leave Cuba soon?” she asked.

“My brother-in-law’s family is trying to get them out, but it takes time.”

“I will pray for them,” she said.

The smell of fried ripe plantains filled the kitchen.

“Pray,” I said, looking down. “I prayed so much during the twelve years that Rio and I were apart, and lost hope so many times.”

“God never abandons his children, Laura. You must have faith. Are your children baptized and confirmed?”

Nelia placed a plate full of fried plantains on the kitchen counter and sat next to me.

“Baptized yes, before Rio left, but then the government began to frown upon people who practiced religion, so no, the children do not know much about it.”

“Don’t they know how to pray?”

“Not really,” I said.

She shook her head in disapproval.

“Laura, your children need God in their lives. Listen, I will talk to my priest and ask him to visit you.”

“Rio will not approve,” I said. “He lost his faith long ago.”

“*Chica,* that doesn’t make sense. How about you, did you also lose your faith?”

I paused for a moment not knowing how to answer that question. During the years I spent without my husband, I had questioned my faith many times. How to keep hope alive for almost twelve years?

“I do believe in God. Of course, I do,” I said. Not exactly responsive to what Nelia had asked me, but that was all I was willing to share.

“Then it’s settled. I will talk to my priest and give him your address. Expect a visit from him.”

“But what about Rio?” I asked.

“He will have to understand that the children have the right to decide what is best for themselves. They will not be able to do this if they are not exposed to the word of God. No matter what Rio thinks, you owe this to your children.”

I nodded, unsure of what Rio would say once he found out. I decided not to tell him. Even if it was not a good idea to start hiding things from him so soon after we had restarted our life together, Nelia was right.

When the children returned from trick-or-treating, each carried a bag full of candies. How could total strangers give candy to children they did not know? This taught me a great deal about the generosity of my new country. What happened next taught me something else.

“Children, do not eat any candy until we examine what you brought,” said Nelia. “Come on, pour the candy on the table.”

Lynette was about to place a piece of chocolate in her mouth, but when she heard Nelia, her eyes opened wide and she put it down quickly.

"Throw away any unwrapped candy and check the wraps for any tears," Nelia said.

I looked at her with inquisitive eyes. Later, she explained that razor blades had been found inside candy in other cities.

"Do you think someone would do that in Tampa?" I asked.

"I don't think so," she said. "But you can never be too careful."

The children spread the candy on the table and I sadly observed as the unwrapped pieces, candy that could possibly be good, were thrown in the garbage.

After the sorting ended, I helped Nelia set the long table in her formal dining room for dinner. Lynette and Gustavo went to the living room with Nelia's children, yet Tania stayed in the kitchen with me, standing in a corner, her face sweaty from the mask she had worn. Her blue overalls and long, light brown hair made her look like a country girl.

I approached Tania while trying to stay out of Nelia's way as she walked in and out of the kitchen carrying food to the dining room. I wanted to help Nelia with the food, but she insisted I had done enough by assisting her with setting the table.

"Did you enjoy yourself?" I asked Tania.

She shrugged.

"It's for children. I'm too old for that," she said.

"It's a new experience. Did you get a lot of candy?"

"Yes. You want one?"

"No, let's wait until after dinner. But thank you for offering." I paused for a moment and caressed her hair. "I love you," I added.

She did not answer. She hardly did when I told her how much I loved her. Instead, she would look the other way or ask me to leave her alone. I did not know how to make my daughter love me. She was only a few months away from her sixteenth birthday and things were not getting any better between us. She did not understand that no one would ever love her as much as I did.

“Dinner is ready!” Nelia announced from the dining room. “Come on, kids. Wash your hands and come over.”

I had lived in the United States for several months, but I could not manage to see a table full of food without thinking about my family in Cuba.

I made sure my children and I served ourselves only what we were going to eat to avoid throwing away food. My two younger kids looked happy. Tania, not so much, but I could see she was enjoying the red beans, white rice, pork, and plantains.

Our family was beginning to make Tampa its home, and I could not be thankful enough for our new friends and for this city, so much smaller than Miami, that had already started to warm our hearts.

Chapter 7 - Communion

I asked Nelia not to speak with the priest right away. I wanted to give Rio time to adapt to being a married man with a family. After so many years alone, this was no easy task. He was used to going to bars after work, and not discussing decisions with anyone. Now he could not do any of these things, and dealing with teenagers proved more difficult than he had expected.

Lynette, my middle child, had always slept in my bedroom when we were in Cuba and was resentful she could not do it anymore. Gustavo wanted all of his father's attention, and Tania was cautious about getting close to her father, or to anyone else. She concentrated on her writing and her studies. Rio wanted her to be more engaged with the family and would make funny faces at her when she was studying. She would raise her brow, smile briefly, and return to her work.

So many times I tried to break the wall Tania had erected between herself and those around her. I thought she blamed me for the years we'd spent away from her father, and perhaps she had not forgiven me for attempting against my life when she was a little girl. I never asked her. It was embarrassing to bring up the subject. I had always been the one to bring hope to others, and to remember that my depression had led me to that day made me feel ashamed of myself. To cope, I convinced myself that she had forgotten about the worst day of my life—not very smart of me to think that events like that can be erased as simply as erasing numbers from a whiteboard.

Her coldness towards me saddened me, but I had other pressing issues, like my children's future, that occupied my mind. I could not change the past, and the last thing I wanted was to baby her. She was almost an adult and needed to understand that life was not perfect, that her future depended on her ability to adapt to situations. People in the United States called this "tough love."

The children were growing fast and becoming accustomed to their new country, while the adults, especially my mother-in-law and me, kept Cuba in our hearts. People in Cuba said often "a man should never forget the place where he is from." My mother-in-law, Rio, and I lived by these words, but not the children. Every time I brought up the subject, Tania would tell me:

"Can you stop talking about Cuba? What's the point? Haven't you suffered enough?"

She had a point. Rio used to think that Cuba had a mysterious hold over the people who lived there, that it did not matter how far Cubans were from their homeland, Cuba would always be in their hearts. Some of our friends had virtually created shrines to Cuba, from paintings to statutes of the Virgin of Charity, to collections of old coins. Remembering Cuba healed and hurt all at the same time.

Although Tania was adjusting well to her new country, she started to compare how she and some of her friends lived. They had cars, wore nice clothes, and lived in better houses. I insisted that I did not want them to place value on material things.

"Having a family and loving each other is the most important thing," I would tell them. This concept was difficult to explain to teenagers who wanted to be like their friends. One day, disregarding all I had taught her, Tania approached her father and said:

"Dad, can you buy me a car?"

I stared at her to get her attention, but she evaded me.

"Wait a minute!" I said sternly. "We can hardly afford our house payments, and you want a car?"

She crossed her arms, gave me a cold look, and stormed out of the kitchen.

Tania had always been a resourceful girl who fought for what she wanted. The next day, when she came home from school, she dropped off her books on the dining room table and ran to her grandmother, who sat in the backyard reading a letter from her sister.

"Grandma!" she yelled. "Let me show you something."

She kissed her on the cheek and embraced her. She always hugged and kissed her grandmother with a tenderness I wished she would show toward me.

Through the open windows, I could hear their conversation.

"What are those books?" her grandmother asked.

"I'm selling Avon products," she said with a big smile as she turned the colorful pages, full of pictures of lipsticks, eye-shadow, creams, and other beauty products.

"Aren't you too young for that?" her grandmother asked.

Tania grabbed a chair and sat next to her.

"Well, let me explain. I can't be a seller because I'm not eighteen, but the mom of one of my friends sells Avon products for a commission. If I sell them for her, she will give me a cut. Easy money!"

I did not like what I was hearing. I washed my hands and joined Tania and her grandmother in the backyard. I embraced my daughter, and she stayed still. “No hugs for me?”

She looked away and began to bite her fingers. I did not insist.

“What are you selling?” I asked.

“Cosmetics,” she said, avoiding my eyes.

“I agree with your grandmother,” I said. “You’re too young. Besides, you need to focus on school. That should be your only priority.”

“I *will* continue to focus on my studies,” she said, rolling her eyes. “But I can do both.”

“You don’t have enough time,” I said. “You know perfectly well that I have big dreams for my family. I want you to become successful in this country.”

She took a deep breath.

“I do have time!” she complained.

“Your grades are not what they used to be in Cuba.”

Tania wrinkled her eyebrows and stared at me.

“Really, Mom? Do you think my grades can be the same when you took me to a place where I don’t understand what my teachers say? I’m spending hours translating stuff. Then in class, I have to help my sister, and while I’m helping her, I can’t pay attention to my teacher.”

Lynette, being a year younger than Tania, was a year behind her in school when we were in Cuba, but when we arrived in the United States, I felt it was better to have both of them in the same grade. This may have been a disservice to Lynette, who had basically missed an entire grade. Tania knew how important it was for me that she help her sister.

“Well, that means you have to focus on learning English. That should take up all of your time.”

Tania shook her head and took a deep breath.

"You're always complaining that I'm shy, that I need to get out of my shell, right?" she asked, gesticulating with her hands.

"Yes. What does that have to do with this?"

"Well, if I sell Avon, I will have to talk to people. I can kill two birds with one stone. It also allows me to speak in English and to be more outgoing."

Her argument seemed convincing.

"You always have an answer for everything," I said.

My mother-in-law had been quietly watching the exchange. She folded the letter from her sister and said, "Laura, Tania is a good girl. Don't you trust her?"

I remained silent for a moment and looked at Mayda with frustration, my eyebrows pulled down together. I was upset she had intervened, but then, after thinking about it, I realized she had a point. I took a deep breath, turned to Tania and held her hands between mine.

"Of course I trust her," I said. "How couldn't I? She is my oldest daughter, my confidant all those years I was alone in Cuba." I paused and caressed Tania's hair.

The next day, Tania began to sell Avon at school. She was very good at it, and before long, she had been able to save over $600. Her persistence impressed me. She wanted to own a car, like many of her schoolmates. However, we could not afford her insurance.

"I will get a job to pay for my insurance!" Tania announced one Saturday morning during breakfast, as the curious faces of her brother and sister watched the exchange.

"You will not get a job," said her father immediately.

"But my friends have jobs, Dad! Why can't I?"

"Because I need you to concentrate on your studies. That is the most important thing. Your mother and I want you to have a good future," he said.

"Yes, I know, I know," she said dismissively while she rolled her eyes. "You've said it a thousand times. You want me to be successful."

Tania arose from the table abruptly without finishing her milk and toast. "I'm going to my bedroom. I'm not hungry."

Her father pointed at the chair with an angry look. "You will sit down and eat your breakfast!"

Tania stared at her father angrily, and he reciprocated. I held my breath for a moment when I saw her cross her arms. I looked at her trying to get her attention. At last, our eyes met and I shook my head from side to side. She then took a deep breath, looked at her plate, sat down, and began to eat her sunny-side-up egg and toast. After finishing her meal, she got up and looked at her father.

"Happy?" she asked defiantly.

It was the first time she had spoken to her father like that, and I was afraid of Rio's reaction. He did not answer, but continued to look at her seriously.

"You may go to your bedroom now," he said.

She stormed out of the room, but later, after I talked to her and she had a chance to think about what had happened, she apologized to her father.

The kids had quickly learned that they should not test their father's temper, and for the most part, they tried not to upset him. Even if they became angry at him, their anger would diffuse quickly, perhaps because he tried so hard to make them like him. Rio always looked for ways to bring excitement into their lives, like the day he taught them how to target shoot with a pellet gun in the backyard. I didn't like seeing my children with a gun, but I understood that, for our marriage to work, there would have to be compromises. The pellet gun was one of many.

Chapter 7 - Communion

When Rio was happy, he turned into a child. He would chase the kids around the house, tickle me, make funny faces, wear a wig and dark glasses, anything to make them laugh. And for a moment, he would forget about his past and the unexpected calls that made me wonder if his previous life had caught up with him. But our lives were never short of complications.

One rainy September morning, we were having breakfast when we heard someone crying outside our kitchen door. I rushed to the door thinking it was a child, but when I looked down, sitting on the last of the three concrete steps that led to our kitchen from our side yard was a puppy. The loving creature had short white hair, brown spots, and sad light brown eyes. Tania picked him up and cradled him in her arms. He was shivering when she brought him inside.

"He's cold," she said. "Hurry, bring him some milk. He's hungry."

Rio had finished his breakfast and was about to smoke a cigarette, but instead, he put it down in the ashtray and walked towards Tania.

"If you feed it, it will want to stay," said Rio.

Tania caressed the puppy and Lynette and Gustavo gathered around her and caressed him too.

"Please, Dad, let us keep him," Tania said.

I poured some milk into an aluminum container and placed it on the floor, disregarding what Rio had said. Tania put the puppy down, and he immediately ran to the container and drank all the milk. He stayed there, licking the empty container and shaking. I poured some more milk, and after he finished, Tania picked him up.

"Dad, can we keep him?" she asked.

Rio did not realize the importance of Tania's question. This was a breakthrough. Until then, I wondered if she really cared about anything or anyone—

other than her grandmother. I looked at Rio with pleading eyes.

"We have so many expenses," he said. He looked at the puppy, trying to maintain his tough demeanor, but the slight inclination of his head, the way he pressed his lips closed together, and the hint of compassion I saw in his eyes conveyed a different, softer part of him.

"I will give him part of my food," said Gustavo. The girls echoed his words.

"Let the kids keep the dog," said Mayda.

"Please, Dad," begged Lynette.

Rio took a deep breath.

"Fine," he said.

The eyes of my three kids lit up, and they all rushed to their father and hugged him. As they stood around him, Tania holding the puppy with one arm and embracing her dad with the other, Rio looked at me, shook his head and shrugged. I smiled at him and just like that, Danny entered our lives.

A couple of weeks passed. We had just finished dinner that Thursday evening when we heard the doorbell. Our dog started to bark and Rio opened the door to let him out to the backyard.

"Gustavo, can you see who's there?" I asked my son.

"Why me?" he protested.

"Stop arguing with your mother and do what she says," said Rio, as he lit a More Menthol cigarette. He sat by our dining room table, while the girls, my mother-in-law and I cleared the plates and the cups.

Rio looked tired and frustrated. I thought lack of sleep was to blame. Sometimes, he worked third shift, but on this particular day, someone had called in sick and he had to be at the 7-Eleven before 7 a.m.

Gustavo walked to the front door and opened it. I heard a male voice ask in broken Spanish, "Is your mom in?"

"Who is it, Gustavo?" I asked.

"I don't know. He wants to talk to you."

When Rio heard that a "he" wanted to see me, he got up and rushed to the front door.

"Go back in, Gustavo," he commanded, "I will talk to him."

I stopped clearing the table, and as I walked towards the front door, I heard Rio say, "No, we are not interested."

He was about to close the door on the man's face when the stranger explained: "Wait, one of your friends sent me! I am here to see your wife, Laura."

"My wife?" Rio asked.

By the time Rio asked that question, I was already behind him. I went around Rio and noticed that the visitor was dressed in black, with a white collar.

"You must be Father Stevens," I said in Spanish. "I was expecting you."

Rio looked at me with inquisitive eyes.

"Please Father, come in and make yourself at home," I said, swinging the door open.

Rio got out of the way and reluctantly let Father Stevens in.

"Please sit down," I said, pointing to a faded, floral-print sofa placed by one of the windows next to the front door. "Let me bring you some coffee."

"Oh, please don't bother. I know you have to work tomorrow, so this is a short visit."

Rio kept staring at me, trying to grab my attention, but I purposely ignored him. I sat on one of the two rocking chairs in our living room. Rio remained standing.

"I am here about the children," said Father Stevens.

"What about the children?" Rio asked.

"I am one of the priests at St. Joseph's Church. We have a program for children like yours, who have not had religion in their lives. If they have not been baptized, we baptize them and then prepare them for communion."

"We are not interested," said Rio, raising his eyebrows and again trying to get my attention. "They are busy enough with school and trying to learn English. That should be their priority."

"They also need God in their lives," said Father Stevens.

Rio took a step towards Father Stevens, and his body tensed as he stared into the priest's eyes with a scolding look.

"Father, don't come into my house and tell me what my children need or don't need," Rio said, raising his voice in anger.

I moved closer to Rio and grabbed him by his arm.

"Father, would you excuse my husband and me for a minute?" I said.

Rio turned his head towards me and stared at me with piercing eyes.

"Of course," said Father Stevens.

"I'll be right back, Father. Rio, could you come with me?"

"There's nothing to discuss," said Rio.

I could feel his eyes on me, but I evaded them this time and smiled apologetically to Father Stevens.

"Please, Rio. This is important."

When I pronounced the last word, I tried to pull Rio towards me. At first, he refused to move. I was not sure what to do and felt a knot in my stomach. I smiled at Father Stevens again.

"Please make yourself at home, Father."

I let go of Rio's arm and began to walk towards the rear of the house. Rio shook his head and took a deep breath.

"Excuse me," he said angrily, and followed me to my mother-in-law's bedroom. She was still in the kitchen washing dishes and did not ask any questions when we passed by, even though she knew exactly what was going on.

Once Rio was in her bedroom, he closed the door behind him. He then crossed his arms and gave me an unflinching look.

"Are you serious, Laura? Why didn't you discuss this with me?"

I answered, evading his eyes. "I knew you would not approve."

"And yet, you defied me?"

I nodded and this time, I looked at him with pleading eyes and caressed his arms.

"Yes, Rio, I did," I said, calmly. "I knew what you were going to say. I understand that your experiences at the orphanage were disappointing and made you angry and distrusting of churches. You have to give your children the opportunity to decide what's best for them."

"Is that what you are doing?" he said. "Or are you just forcing religion down their throats?"

The veins in his neck bulged when he said this.

"No, that is not what I'm doing." I said. "I am teaching them now what I was not able to teach them when we lived in Cuba. When they are adults, they can decide whether to follow those teachings or not."

"I want to save them the disappointment, Laura, of learning that sometimes, no matter how hard they pray, life can screw with them the way it screwed with me!"

I crossed my arms this time.

"Oh, so is that the problem? I don't think *you* understand," I said, raising my eyebrows. "Do you realize that faith is what kept me going for almost twelve years?" I paused for a few seconds to consider carefully what I was about to say next. I did not want to hurt him, or disregard what he went through at the orphanage or during the years we spent apart.

I looked down for a moment, then moved my head slightly upward. Our eyes met.

"Every time I thought I could not continue to raise three children on my own, in a country with no means to do it, *that* belief in something bigger than all of us kept me going, Rio," I said, calmly. "Unfortunately, I could not teach it to them. I didn't want them to be different than the other children, but now I can. You cannot take it away from them."

Rio stayed silent for a moment, and then took a step closer to me.

"So, let me get this straight. My opinion doesn't matter. Is that right?" he asked.

I did not want to fight with him, but there was a reality he needed to consider. For years, he was only in their lives over the telephone or through letters. It was me who changed their diapers, who took them to doctors, who worked twelve hours a day to put food on the table when Rio hardly sent me any money. Deep down, even if I acted as if we both had the same right over our children, I felt I knew what was best for them—yet I realized that our children needed both of us, so I refrained from saying what I was thinking.

"It is not that," I said. "I know you love our children, but you're too hurt to see clearly in this situation. Please, let me do this for them. They stand to gain more than they stand to lose."

A long silence followed. He took a deep breath.

"I do not agree with this, Laura. I think this is a mistake." His frustration was palpable. "I'm already too busy and now you want to take the kids away from me during the little time I have them on the weekends?"

I drew my eyebrows together in disbelief.

"Is that the real reason why you don't want them to go to church?"

He tapped his right index finger against his thigh and shook his head.

"You know," he said. "I give up! Do whatever you want, just don't ask me to agree with it."

I reached for his hand.

"Please, understand," I pleaded.

"I'm done. There's nothing to discuss," he said, and stormed out the door that led to the backyard, waving his right arm in dismissal.

It was our first real disagreement. Rio had told me about the losses of his father and his older brother when he was a child, the years he had spent at an orphanage ran by priests when his mother's pain was so great that, following these unexpected deaths, she could no longer be a mother to him. He also told me about the many times the priest who ran the school had thrown a bucket of dirty water on the floor after Rio had finished mopping it.

His mother had visited him at the orphanage occasionally. Rio prayed she would take him back home. But when she didn't, not even after she traded the black dress she'd worn for months for one of a floral print, he stopped praying. He stopped believing. I understood his sadness and hoped that one day he would regain his faith, but his experiences were his alone, not our children's.

Despite Rio's reluctance, I signed the children up for catechism classes, and they began to prepare for communion.

Chapter 8 - Our New Life

Calls to Cuba were expensive, so I would tell my sister through letters, mostly, about our new life and the gifts the children received from the church and friends. I was touched by the generosity of the people in Tampa. Their kindness made me fall in love with the city.

The composition of Tampa's population, working families and a growing middle class, attracted me. It had two universities—the University of Tampa and the University of South Florida—and a small downtown that was bordered by the Hillsborough River. The University of Tampa, previously the Tampa Bay Hotel—topped by Moorish minarets, domes, and cupolas—was the most iconic symbol of the city.

I loved the times that Rio drove the children and me through the two university campuses.

"I want you to study at a university like this one, get a degree, and become successful," I would tell my children. "There is nothing more important than an education."

Through friends, Tania met a writer, Louise, a middle-age woman who was battling a deadly disease. Tania had shared some of her stories, written in Spanish, with her, and Louise, touched by them, had encouraged her to keep writing. During Louise's second visit to the house, she brought Tania a journal. My daughter treasured this gift and hoped to be able to write in English one day.

Louise gave Tania a used record player with a collection of long-play records. It was in better condition than one we had received from another neighbor, which we then donated to one of Tania's friends.

The girls loved to dance and listen to American music, something they had not been able to do freely in Cuba, as it was prohibited. I enjoyed watching the happiness on the girls' faces, but most of all, I liked to see Tania laugh... yet her resentment toward me remained unchanged.

During our first few months in Tampa, I changed jobs frequently. Unable to keep up with the volume of work I had at the hotel, I looked for another job and found one preparing food for the airplanes. But after having taught for so many years, making the transition to a production line proved difficult. I was fired after the first couple of months. Finally, someone told me about a job working as a front-desk clerk at a hospital. My English was not yet strong enough, so I bought used books and tapes to continue to refresh my knowledge and began to practice my pronunciation in the evenings, after everyone had gone to bed.

"My name is Laura. What is your name? How are you?" I would repeat and have full conversations with myself. My efforts paid off, and I was hired.

Over time, we began to establish other connections that would allow Rio to find a job at a glass company. The pay was much higher than at 7-Eleven. The day he was hired, he came home with a radiant smile on his face and shared the news with his mother.

"Working with glass? Are you crazy?" Mayda said.

"It pays well, Mom. We have a big family."

"I can't believe you are risking your life for money," she said, crossing her arms. "I don't know what I would do if something happened to you. It is not worth the risk!"

"Mom, don't worry. I will be fine," he said.

"Grandma, Dad is strong," said Gustavo. "He can handle it."

Mayda looked at Rio with an angry expression.

"I'm going to bed. Nobody ever listens to what I say. It's like I don't exist. And don't bother calling me for dinner. I won't eat tonight."

Mayda walked away. Soon after, she started to skip meals and get up late. But Rio's job was not the only reason for the changes she was experiencing. She missed Cuba and her family, and we failed to assess the toll the move from Cuba had taken on her mental health.

We all insisted that she needed to eat and to become part of family activities. Yet, she refused to listen and fell deeper into depression—a depression we mistook for stubbornness. Danny, our beloved pet, would try to cheer her up. He would sit by her side and lick her hands, but not even his affection helped her.

Mayda seldom left the house, no matter how much we insisted that new surroundings would help her. With two better-paying jobs, Rio would surprise us occasionally with trips to restaurants. Nothing fancy: pizza, burgers, or fried seafood. Rio's pleas to his mother to join us would often be discarded. It was as if she was waiting for a call that never came.

We lived a simple life: working, helping the children with homework, visiting the parks on weekends. Rio assigned chores to the children, from mowing the lawn to washing dishes. One day, seeing the overgrown yard of an elderly neighbor, Rio made the children accompany him to the woman's house. Rio had pushed the lawn mower for an entire block until he arrived at the old frame house where the woman lived. He waited outside with the girls and asked Gustavo to knock on her door.

"My dad, my sisters, and I will mow your lawn for free," said Gustavo in broken English when the frail, white-haired woman opened the door.

"No, that's okay. Leave it like that," she said.

"Don't worry. We won't charge you. My dad says we should help our neighbors. We are going to start now, okay?"

The woman smiled, held my brother's hands between hers, and said, "God bless you and your family."

It was a hot day, and Rio made sure that everyone had their turn at mowing the yard, even the girls who used their hands to pull the tall weeds from the side of the house when it was not their turn to mow. The children returned home with sweaty faces and blisters on their hands, but Rio insisted that this lesson would teach them to be better citizens and to care about those less fortunate.

From the beginning, Rio had not allowed them to watch Spanish channels, and this discipline allowed them to pick up English more quickly than some of the other kids.

They were growing so fast. Gustavo was as tall as me, but then, I was short by United States standards, only five feet and a couple of inches.

Two weeks before our first Christmas together, Rio drove the children to a house in the Town and Country area that drew big crowds because its owner decorated it lavishly for the holidays. We had never seen anything like it. So many colorful lights, an electric train looping around a handsomely decorated Christmas tree, a huge snowman, and a life-sized baby Jesus surrounded by a Nativity set. When I saw the families lining up to see it, I felt tears welling up.

"Look, Dad!" Gustavo and Lynette kept saying. Tania did not say anything, but her eyes were glued to the window as Rio drove by the house multiple times.

After the drive, Rio decided to take the children to the store to look at Christmas trees. As soon as I saw the prices, I shook my head.

"We cannot afford it. It is not just the tree, but the decorations, the lights... It is too much money for something that we will use a few days," I said.

Rio did not disagree, but his disappointment was evident as we passed by the checkout line empty-handed, when other families were lined up to purchase trees and Christmas decorations.

Rio would not give up so easily. The weekend before Christmas, the children and I were watching television, when our front door opened, and moments later, Rio entered carrying a big pine Christmas tree. He was glowing with happiness.

"Did you buy it?" I asked. "It must have cost a fortune."

He shook his head.

"So if you did not buy it, where did you find it?"

"I didn't want the kids to be without a tree during their first Christmas," he said with a big mischievous smile, like a kid who had done something bad. "There is a parcel of land in Drew Park, near the airport. It is full of pine trees. I looked for the nicest one I could find and cut it!"

"You did what?" I asked. "Isn't that illegal?"

"I think the lot belongs to the airport," he said. "They won't miss it. If anything, I may have done them a favor. One less tree to cut the day they decide to expand. I heard they had plans."

"I can't believe you risked going to jail to please your children," I said.

He shrugged, smiled, and did a little victory dance. I was not happy. His actions were inconsistent with the values I wanted my children to have. Later, in the privacy of our room, I shared my concern with him.

"I only wanted them to be happy," he said.

"Material things don't necessarily make a person happy, not in the long run. Love, family, hard work. Those are things that matter. I know you are doing the best you can, and I thank you. We just need to think of how our decisions will impact them later."

He inhaled deeply and then exhaled.

"You are asking a lot from me. Let me enjoy this," he said, and went out of the room.

The children helped their father take the tree and a stand he had purchased to a corner of the room. Once they had positioned it and secured it, Danny began making circles around it. The next day, when Tania's writer friend learned about the tree, she talked to friends and brought us used decorations and lights. She even helped us decorate it. It looked beautiful!

On Christmas Day, as my children sat around the tree opening presents, I could not imagine being any happier than I was, so I thanked God for my family and the life we lived.

Chapter 9 - First Date

Lynette and I arrived from school and found my grandmother washing dishes in the kitchen and my brother watching *Star Trek* reruns in the living room. Noticing he had not changed from his school clothes, I reminded him.

"Stop telling me what to do!" he said. "You're not my mother."

"But I am seventeen, much older than you," I said. "You know that Dad will be mad if he sees you in school clothes when he arrives from work."

"So what? I'm fourteen years old. I'm a man and can make my own decisions. I won't change."

"It's your funeral," I said, and walked away.

More than two years had passed since our arrival to the United States, and our English was improving each day—so much so that sometimes, especially when we wanted to hide something from the adults, we would speak to each other in broken English.

During the time we had been in the United States, I thought a lot about my boyfriend and my friends in Cuba and wondered what had happened when they learned I had left and would never return.

I had made new friends, not many, but I was starting to get used to my new life. I liked Jefferson High School. The teachers were great and the school was cleaner and newer than any school I had attended in Cuba.

I was in my senior year, and after hours of hard work, my grades had drastically improved. I had gone from making mostly Cs and Ds in the tenth grade to mostly As.

I had not dated anyone in the United States. I was too busy between my writing and my school. I missed playing the piano like I did when we lived in Cuba. It had taken a long time for my mother to find a piano, but on the day she came home with one, I realized she had performed another miracle. It was in desperate need of tuning and had broken keys, but I'd loved it. I hoped to be able to have one again one day.

My father had taught me how to drive, but unlike many of my friends, I did not own a car and not being able to afford one or the nicer clothes many of the girls in my class wore made me feel less confident, like I did not belong.

I still had nightmares, less often than before, but I did not tell anyone, not even my sister. They were always the same. I would see myself inside a box that kept getting smaller and smaller until I could no longer breathe and I would wake up sweating, my heart pounding. It had been about ten years since they'd started. I thought it was my body's way of reminding me there was something wrong with me, that I was not normal.

"Grandma, I have great news!" said my sixteen-year-old sister, as she kissed and hugged my grandmother. "I'm in love!"

My grandmother stopped what she was doing and dried her hands. Then, she turned to my sister and looked at her inquisitively.

"In love?" she asked. "You're just a child. What do you know about love?"

"Oh, Grandma, you don't understand. He is so handsome! He is as white as a ghost, has black hair and a small black mustache."

"Dear God! Are you in love with Hitler?" asked my grandmother as I was sipping some water and I almost spit it out from the laughter.

"No, I am not in love with Hitler. He is the most handsome boy I have ever seen."

My grandmother shook her head, and then her eyes drifted. I imagined what she was thinking when my sister mentioned the word "love."

Just a week before, she had received a letter from her sister. "Dear sister," the letter stated,

It is very hard for me to write these words. I struggled with the idea for days, but I came to the conclusion that you needed to know. It is not fair to keep it from you any longer.

With a heavy heart, I regret to tell you that your dear husband passed away in his sleep, shortly after you left. Be comforted in the fact he did not suffer and that he is with God now. He loved you very much, and I am sure he will wait for you in Heaven. I miss you, Mayda.

Your house stayed empty for a while, but now, a couple moved in. Probably revolutionaries. It saddens me getting up each morning and not seeing you working in your rose garden.

Our family is fine, but now that you left so suddenly, my daughter and grandchildren have started to talk about leaving. I am fearful that when my time comes, I will die alone. Only time will tell. I just want what is best for them, and if my daughter decides to leave, I will not stop her.

A hug from my family and me. I hope that we can see each other again one day.

Chapter 9 - First Date

For three days, my grandmother had hardly left her room.

Now she took a deep breath and approached Lynette. "Child, take your time," she said. "There will be plenty of handsome boys to choose from. You look beautiful, like I did when I was your age. Let them come to you."

"But he did, Grandma," said Lynette, looking at her then sighing. "He invited me to the prom. I am so happy!"

Lynette embraced herself and looked up.

"The prom?" asked my grandmother. "What does that mean?"

"It's a school party," I said.

"Now I know my first word in English," said my grandmother. "Weird name for a party."

She paused for a moment and turned towards me.

"Tania, do you know this prince charming?" she asked.

I shook my head and rolled my eyes.

"Lynette please, focus on what's important," Grandma said. "You can wait a while longer to start going out with boys. Besides, don't you know your father?"

"Yes, Grandma. I know Dad, but *that* is where you come in."

"Excuse me?" asked my grandmother, crossing her arms.

"Yes, my little Grandma. I need you to convince Dad. Please help me!"

"I cannot get between you and your father. You know how angry he gets when I get involved."

"One last time, please. I promise. I will not ask you for any favors ever again. Do you know how hard it is for a Cuban refugee, like me, to be invited to the prom by someone who speaks perfect English? But he *did* invite me! I cannot turn him down. That would be unforgivable."

Gustavo, who had lowered the volume on the television to hear our conversation, walked into the kitchen.

“You’re not going anywhere. Dad will not let you!” he said.

“Don’t you have some homework to do, pinhead?” Lynette asked. “Or better yet, go play with your little toys.”

“I’m a man. I don’t play with toys.”

Lynette continued to make fun of him, until he stormed out of the kitchen.

Later, when my parents sat at the dinner table, my sister told Mom about the party. As Gustavo suspected, my father said no. Gustavo stared at my sister and raised his eyebrows.

“Rio, you need to let the girls enjoy themselves,” my grandmother said, as she served the spaghetti and meatballs.

We all held our breath and noticed the angry look my father gave her. He scratched his head and tapped his index finger on the table. We knew what would come next.

“Mom,” said my father, “I’m sick and tired of you believing that you can tell me how to raise my kids.”

My grandmother’s eyes glistened with tears. “Your kids?” said Grandma. “Do you think I don’t care about them?” She paused and stared at my father angrily. “I don’t want to say hurtful things to you, son, but I helped feed *your* children for many years when you hardly sent them any money. I’m sorry, I can’t do this! I’m going to bed.”

My father closed his eyes, massaged his temples, and slammed the table with his fist. He then got up and stormed out to the backyard, his pack of cigarettes and a lighter in his hand.

Chapter 9 - First Date

"Kids, finish serving yourselves," Mom said. "Lynette, next time, wait for dinner to be over before you bring up subjects like these. You know that your father is trying to protect you. Let me try to fix this, so we can all eat in peace."

She followed my father outside and was gone for a while. When they returned, Dad went into Grandma's bedroom and my mother approached Lynette.

"Your father will allow you to go, but you need to bring Tania as a chaperone," she said and took a deep breath.

Moments later, Dad walked out of Grandma's bedroom and did not say a word or look at anyone. He scowled and shook his head while pacing towards his room. He did not eat that night.

When Lynette's date heard I was going, he asked one of his friends to be my date. However, Mom heard that we both were going to the dance with boys, and as instructed by our father, she had to accompany us. We would be the only girls to bring their mothers to the prom that year.

My mother failed to realize at first that we would both need nice dresses for the party, and when she did, she knew we could not afford them. She talked to friends who talked to other friends. Finally, the wife of a well-known Spanish radio personality invited us to her house and volunteered to make our dresses. My mother did not want to take advantage of her generosity, but the woman insisted. She'd never had children of her own, and she explained to my mother that doing this would help her experience what it was like to be a mother. We began to visit her more frequently after that, as she started to work on our dresses. During each visit, she welcomed us with a wide, friendly smile, soft drinks and cookies.

At last, the dresses were finished, both long, mine pink with a V-neck and ruffles, and my sister's, beige and draped.

The night I met Phil, my date for the prom, I was seventeen. I still had not dated anyone in the United States. He and my sister's boyfriend visited us unexpectedly. They arrived wearing musky cologne and dressed in nice polo shirts and pleated pants. My father opened the door, and when they mentioned they had come to visit us, he shook his head and yelled, "Laura, please come here and take care of this! I'm going to work in the back. You stay with the girls."

We came into the living room wearing white shorts and t-shirts. Lynette's boyfriend introduced me to Phil. He clearly did not know whether to kiss me or shake my hand, but when it became clear to him, from my expression and body movements, that kissing was the standard protocol, he awkwardly approached me and kissed me on the cheek. Later, I would learn, to my embarrassment, that kissing on the cheeks was not truly the standard practice in the United States.

We both acted nervously around each other, my hands sweaty, my eyes evading his. At first sight, he appeared to me like someone who spent his entire day reading: thick glasses, smart eyes, and a forced bad-boy smile I found amusing.

"Hi, I'm Tania," I said.

"I'm Phil."

We stood there, looking at each other awkwardly.

"Can I sit down?" he asked.

I opened my eyes wide and said, with a nervous smile, "Oh, I'm so sorry! Sure."

Lynette and her boyfriend had already taken the loveseat, so Phil and I sat on the sofa. After saying hello to the boys, my mother sat on a chair in the living room to supervise the visit.

"What's going on?" Lynette's boyfriend asked her in English, as he looked at my mother and then back at Lynette.

"Don't mind my mother," she said. "It's my Dad. He's strict."

Her boyfriend shrugged.

"Do you boys want something to drink?" my mother asked.

"No, thank you," they both answered.

"So, where do you go to school?" Phil asked me, even though he knew the answer.

"Jefferson, and you?"

"Tampa Bay Tech," he said.

"You like it?" I asked.

"I do," he said. "So, someone told me you just came from Cuba a couple of years ago. Is that true?"

"Yes, I'm a Cuban refugee," I answered.

He smiled. "I left Cuba when I was four years old," he said.

"Really?" I asked.

My eyes opened wide. It was the first time that a boy who had been in the United States for so many years had talked to me. That made me feel special. The group of Cubans who had come from the Mariel boatlift had gained a negative reputation because of the number of people whom Castro had taken out of jails to join that exodus.

"My father was a political prisoner," he said.

"A political prisoner?" I said, opening my eyes wide. "That's awful."

"It was," he said, as he adjusted his glasses. "I still remember the day he was taken to jail."

"It must have been difficult for you and your mom to witness that."

He nodded. "I was only four, but I closed my fists tightly and hit one of the officers who was taking him. The officer was a big guy. At the time, he looked like a green giant to me because he was wearing a green uniform and was taller than my father. He pushed me away. I fell and began to cry, out of frustration."

"I am so sorry," I said, rubbing my legs nervously, wondering what he would think if he knew that my father, at one point in his life, had defended the revolution that had jailed this boy's father.

Phil's eyes were now focused on my exposed thighs. I tried to pull down the folded fabric, so it would cover more of my legs.

"I should have changed," I said, in a low tone of voice. "But I don't have a lot of clothes. For the last two years, I have been wearing what was donated to us when we arrived."

Phil looked down and seemed pensive for a brief moment.

"I'm sorry," he said. "I didn't mean to . . ."

"I know," I said.

I looked at my mother and realized that she was listening attentively to our conversation, but when our eyes met, she looked the other way.

Judging by my sister's frequent laughs, it was evident that she and her date were discussing less serious matters.

"Do you have any brothers or sisters?" I asked.

"Yes, twin boys," he said.

"I love twins! How old?"

"Five."

We continued to talk about our families and our lives. I learned that Phil worked as a DJ on weekends.

"You, a DJ?" I asked.

"What's wrong? Don't I look like one?"

"No, you don't. You look like my uncle Antonio. He is still in Cuba and wears glasses like you. He is always reading."

"I like to read, but there are things that I like more," he said, and gave me a flirtatious look.

I smiled shyly, looked down, and glanced at my mother.

"So what year did you leave Cuba?" I asked.

"1969, during the Nixon administration."

Phil told me how, the night before he left Cuba, a guard took his favorite toy truck away from him. Four-year-old Phil had begged him to give it back to him, but the guard pushed him away. He remembered that day very clearly. He also explained how important his mother was to him.

"She lost my older brother when he was a baby, and when I was born, she was afraid she would lose me too," Phil said. "As I grew up, she became obsessed with making me happy. She always found a way to give me everything I asked for, if within her means, of course. She's a good mother."

The way he spoke about his mother impressed me.

"What about you? When did you come?" he asked.

"We left Cuba on April 26, 1980, arrived in the United States on April 27th, but our papers were not processed until April 28th. That is the date on our documents."

"My birthday!" he said.

"Really?"

"I'm serious. Maybe you're my birthday present," he said.

"Stop joking! I'm no present," I said, nervously tucking my hair behind my ears.

"Did you know that I went to McFarlane Park in support of the Mariel refugees?

I opened my eyes wide.

"Small world. Why would you care about people like me?"

"Based on what my mother told me, I know what it is like to live in a communist dictatorship. I wanted to help."

I always believed in destiny and that everything happened for a reason. So much connected Phil and me, and I wondered why. I also liked that he seemed genuinely nice, with a touch of bad boy in him.

We enjoyed each other's company that night—so much, that we talked for over an hour, until my father appeared in the living room and announced:

"Visiting hours are over."

Visiting hours? Back then, my father made me feel as if I were in jail.

I could not wait for prom day, even if my mother had to accompany us.

At last, the day of our first party in the United States arrived. I had practiced my dance moves and was ready! Both of our dates arrived with carnations that my mother secured to our dresses with pins after the boys mistakenly thought they would be allowed to fulfill that role.

We rode to the prom in Phil's car, a 1974 Plymouth Duster, with my sister, her boyfriend, and my mother in the back seat, and Phil and me in the front. Phil's car was clean, with a new strawberry air freshener hanging from the rearview mirror. I felt like Cinderella in my new dress, with my prince, Phil, sitting next to me in a white tuxedo.

We were not able to say much on the way to the party. Mom steered the conversation with both boys, trying to learn as much as possible about them, to the point of asking indiscreet questions like, "what do your parents do?" To which Phil responded:

"My mother cleans floors for a living, and my father works at the Tampa Ship Yards."

I could only imagine what she was thinking when she responded, "They do not have a college education?"

I shook my head and took a deep breath.

"No, they had to work at whatever they could find to provide for their kids. She did work for Coca Cola when we were in New York. Those were the good times. I miss New York."

Mother continued to drill the boys about their plans for a formal education, and when neither one gave her a satisfactory answer, she said, "You better start thinking about college now if you want to give your future wives a decent living."

I knew arguing with her was of no use, so when we stopped at a light, I caught Phil's attention and mouthed: "Sorry."

He laughed.

At the entrance of the hotel hall where the party took place, each attendee received a Jefferson High School stuffed monkey. Phil and I gave them to my mother for safekeeping, entered the dark room where the music played, and sat in a corner, next to my mother, to talk. But the music was too loud. My sister and her date began to dance, and following a moment of awkward silence, Phil invited me to the dance floor. When he took my hand, it was like ice.

"Are you nervous?" he asked.

"No, it's cold in here."

We began to dance to a slow song.

"You look very pretty in that dress," he whispered in my ear.

"You look handsome on your tuxedo," I said, shyly. "I like your cologne."

He thanked me, and we continued to dance, but my shoes were uncomfortable, and after a while, I told him that I needed to sit down. Moments later, a blond boy, dressed in a very nice black tuxedo, approached me, grabbed my hand, and said, "May I have this dance?"

I retrieved my hand immediately and asked Phil, "What did he say? Did I understand him right?"

"He wants to dance with you," Phil said, in Spanish.

I felt a knot in my stomach. If this had occurred in Cuba, it would have resulted in a fight, and that is what I was expecting. With an angry look, I said in broken English, "Are you crazy? Don't you see that I came with him?"

The young man apologized and walked away. That was when I noticed that all his friends were laughing at him.

"What was that all about?" I asked Phil.

"He is one of the popular guys here at Jefferson who just made himself look like a fool."

We both laughed.

I did not know it then, but my gesture that night had impressed Phil, making him realize the person I was.

After that night, he asked my mother for permission to visit my house regularly. She reluctantly accepted, and we began to date. During his third visit as an official boyfriend, he walked in with a plastic bag in his hand.

It was Saturday, and my grandmother had come to the door wearing an unbuttoned dress that allowed Phil to see her bra. She asked him to sit down and yelled, "Tania, that guy is here to see you," and before I had a chance to leave my room, she went outside, to the backyard.

My father, my siblings, and my mother were at the store, which left Phil and me alone. He kissed my cheek and asked, "Is your grandmother okay?"

"Why?"

He explained how she had come to the door.

"She is not well," I said. "We are afraid that she is starting to lose her mind. She talks to herself sometimes, you know? She should have never left Cuba."

"Well, enough about your grandmother," he said. "I brought you a gift."

"A gift?"

"Yes, purchased with my own money."

He gave me the bag, and I opened it anxiously. When I examined its contents, I looked at him with a confused expression.

"Are these clothes for me?"

He smiled. "They are. I hope you like them and that they fit you."

"They are beautiful," I said, "but why would you do that?"

"You said that your parents had not been able to buy clothes, so I bought them for you."

My eyes dampened with tears, and before I could contain them, I began to weep.

"Why are you crying?" he asked.

"This is the sweetest thing any boyfriend has ever done for me."

Phil caressed my back. "Come on, you don't have to cry."

Phil came closer to me, kissed me on my cheek softly, and then, our lips met. We kissed passionately for the first time. Everything trembled inside me as we lost ourselves in the moment, our bodies together, and his arms around me bringing me closer to him and pressing his fingers against my skin.

Suddenly, I heard a car park outside, followed by the slamming of doors. I quickly stepped back, still shaken.

"My father is here!" I said. "Let me take these clothes to the back. I don't want him to see them. I also don't want him to know that we are here alone."

I ran to my room leaving Phil in the living room and timed my return, so my father would see me walking from the back of the house when he opened the door.

"Where is your grandmother?" asked my father.

"In the backyard," I said.

My father asked Gustavo to sit with us in the living room, while, he, my mother, and my sister took the groceries out of the car.

"Would you like some help?" Phil asked my father.

"No, thank you," my father said, with a serious expression.

Later that evening, I shared with my mother what Phil had told me about my grandmother.

"She is not well, Tania. We need to take her to a psychiatrist. Something is off."

But for one reason or another, her appointment kept getting postponed. I did not realize then the magnitude of my grandmother's problems. No one did. We were too busy with school, work, learning English, watching television, studying, and trying to make it in America. And we failed to notice just how broken she was.

Chapter 10 - Complications

My oldest daughter was dating this new boy, Phil, the last thing I needed. I had enough with Rio's paranoia about his previous life, his carelessness with our finances, my mother-in-law's mental deterioration, and the separation from my sister. I loved Rio; God knew how much, and I would have done anything for him, but in our situation, to spend over twenty dollars a week on beer and cigarettes or fifty dollars at a restaurant seemed irresponsible.

Once Rio noticed my good money-managing skills, which I had acquired during the years we spent apart, he would give me his check every week. I'd set aside the money for our mortgage and as much as I could for an extra payment. We needed to pay off the house to increase our disposable income. But when Rio did not have the cash, he would pay for his habits with a credit card, and I could never pay off the balances or save money for college. We fought about it many times without recognizing that his dependency on cigarettes and alcohol required treatment. I thought he could just stop doing these things that, he believed, had kept him from losing his mind during the years he was alone.

I felt physically and mentally exhausted trying to keep it all together, telling myself I still had control, when my life was unraveling in front of me. And now my daughter was dating this impulsive boy who liked to play loud music and drive fast cars. He came from a good Christian family, and that comforted me, but I expected someone different for my daughter. Now, I understood how my mother felt when I started to date Rio, someone she considered irresponsible and reckless.

Tania was a smart and responsible girl, but she had inherited her father's stubbornness. When—only months after she and Phil started to date—they told me they wanted to get married, I'd had enough.

"You what?" I asked, trying to keep my voice down, so Rio, who was in the backyard, could not hear us.

We were sitting in the living room, Tania and Phil holding hands on the sofa, me on a rocking chair.

"You're finishing high school. You are two kids. Phil, you only have a part-time job and so do you, Tania. How do you think you are going to support yourselves?"

"I will do whatever I need to do, work more hours, get another job," said Phil.

"And neglect your education?" I said, interlacing my fingers over my head.

Tania crossed her arms.

"We are not kids, Mom! Why are you always treating us like we are?"

"Because you *are* kids," I said angrily.

She had successfully made me lose my patience. I stood up and signaled her to come over.

"The day you have a college education and a decent-paying job, the day that you make me proud to have sacrificed *my* life for *your* future, *that* is the day that you will stop being a child in my eyes!" I said, pointing at her.

She took a few steps back, drew in her eyebrows, and gave me a glaring look.

"You think you know it all and that you have all the answers, but you don't know me, Mom. You never have. I can't wait for the day that I'm out of this house! Phil, stop wasting your time. This conversation is over."

"Tania, you do not speak to your mother like that," I said sternly, pointing at her with my index finger. "Apologize this very moment if you do not want me to suspend Phil's visits for an entire week. Do I make myself clear?"

She stomped her foot in protest and looked at me defiantly. Then, her head turned to Phil whose expression urged Tania to comply.

She raised her arms out of frustration.

"Fine. I apologize, Mother, for wanting to control my own life," she said. "Happy?"

"Phil, please go home now," I said. "Tania needs to think about what happened."

Phil nervously said good-bye to my daughter and kissed her on her cheek. She did not respond, just looked down. As he walked towards the front door, she turned around, glanced at me with a look of defiance, and stormed out of the room. Moments later, I heard her slam the door of her bedroom. I followed her.

"If you break the door, you will pay for it!" I said from outside her bedroom.

She did not answer, but I heard her weeping.

I needed to do something. Knowing this was not going to be the end of this argument, I could not keep what had happened to myself.

Rio was in the room in the back of the house cutting a piece of wood when I found him.

"We need to talk," I said.

He stopped what he was doing and raised his head.

"Is everything okay?"

I shook my head.

"No," I said. "We have a problem. Tania wants to marry this boy, Phil."

"She what?" he said, shrinking his eyes.

"Don't worry, I did not take the news seriously, but I know Tania. I'm afraid this is not going to end here."

"I will talk to that kid," he said. "Who does he think he is? And why didn't he talk to me?"

"He wanted to," I said. "Tania would not let him because she knew what you were going to say. They thought that going through me would change things."

I rested my chin on my hand pensively.

"Maybe . . .," I said, after a brief silence. "You should follow Tania's school bus before going to work, at least for a while. She cannot suspect anything. We have to make sure Phil is not picking her up. Oh my God, I don't know what I would do if she begins to skip school to be with this boy."

Rio shook his head.

"Wait a minute! What role do you think I play here?" he said, gesturing with his hands. "If that Phil places a finger on my daughter, I will kill him! I swear! He doesn't know who he's messing with."

I took a deep breath.

"Stop talking like that! You are not going to kill anyone. Tania loves this boy, and he loves her. That is very clear to me. We need to confront this tactfully."

Rio did not respond, just looked at me, his face contorted with a mixture of anger and preoccupation. The tables had turned, and he had few options. On the next school day, he began to follow Tania's bus before going to his job at the glass company.

Tania did not talk to me for the next couple of days, but after that, she seemed to have gotten over it. At least, that was what I thought.

A few days later, when I was in the kitchen pouring a package of black beans into the pressure cooker, the telephone rang. Rio was not at home. He had left earlier that morning to work an extra shift at the glass company.

I picked up the handset. It was Rio's boss.

"What happened? Is Rio okay?" I asked.

A brief silence followed, and then a deep breath.

"Rio had an accident," he said somberly.

"Oh, my God!" My heart began to beat faster, as I imagined the worst. "Is he okay?"

"He was rushed by ambulance to Tampa General Hospital."

"But, what happened?"

"A pallet of glass fell on his back."

I swallowed and my voice cracked as I asked again: "Is he going to be okay?"

"I am leaving the company in a few minutes and will pick you up. Don't worry. He will be fine," he said unconvincingly.

I thought about Mayda. She had often begged Rio to find a different job, one less dangerous. I decided not to tell her anything until I knew how he was. When I left, I told her we were going to a friend's house and would be gone for a while. She did not suspect anything.

William, Rio's boss, and his wife, Sarah, who also worked in the office, both came to pick me up. Tania volunteered to accompany me.

When we arrived at the hospital, located in Davis Island, near the downtown Tampa area, I left Tania, William, and Sarah in the waiting room and went inside alone. Tania wanted to go with me, but the emergency-room staff would only allow one person in the room.

A nurse led me past several patient beds before getting to Rio's. I felt a knot in my stomach, unsure of what I would find. At last, I saw him. He had a bandaged torso, an IV in his arm, and his eyes closed, but when I approached him, my footsteps awoke him.

"You are here!" Rio said. "Who brought you? How did you find out?"

"William and Sarah picked me up at home. Tania is also here. She was worried."

He nodded in approval.

"Are you in pain?" I asked.

"The nurses are giving me pain medication regularly. I was in a lot more pain when I arrived."

"Will you be able to go home soon?"

"I don't know," he said. "The doctors are doing more tests."

He had just finished saying those words when I saw a nurse come in, followed by Tania.

"There is already a visitor in the room," the nurse told Tania after she saw me. "Only one of you can stay with the patient."

"This is my wife, and she is my daughter," said Rio in broken English. "Can they both stay here for a while?"

The nurse hesitated.

"Only for a little while," she said.

Once the nurse left, Tania carefully approached her father.

"Are you okay, Dad?"

He reached for her hand and placed it between his.

"I will be," he said. "I will be."

Her eyes moistened with tears as she caressed her father's arm. She then rested her head gently over his.

"I'm sorry, Dad," she said.

Chapter 11 - Goodbye

When my mother arrived from work that day, she noticed an envelope on the dining-room table. She glanced at it casually and picked it up, noticing the sender's name and address.

"Your aunt is in Costa Rica!" she announced, as she frantically opened the letter and rushed to her bedroom. I followed her and sat next to her on the bed as she began to read.

It was a short letter, one page. Misty-eyed, Mother covered her mouth as she read. When she finished, she put the sheet down, hugged me, and said:

"At last! They were able to leave Cuba!"

"Are they okay?" I asked.

"Here, read it yourself," she said, her voice cracking.

I began to read.

Dear sister,

Almost two years after you left, we were finally able to leave Cuba. The nightmare is over. I wanted to surprise you, thinking that my stay here would be short, but I have to stay in Costa Rica a little longer than I planned. Things are tough here. We live in a tiny apartment, have not been able to get jobs, but we are together and that is what counts. One of my husband's relatives is helping us with living expenses until the immigration papers are complete and we are able to travel to the United States. I hope to see you soon. I cannot wait to embrace you and the kids again. I miss you all so much.

Love,

Your sister.

My mother was now crying in her typical dramatic way that had made my aunt assert, when we lived in Cuba, that Mother lived in another universe. True, Mother did not share her sister's pragmatism, but she had an inner beauty, one I failed to recognize until much later.

"I can't believe it! I can't believe it! I am so happy!" she said, wiping her tears.

I smiled and patted her on her back, and she embraced me again.

A month later, Aunt Berta called my mother. The day of her trip to Miami had been scheduled. By then, my father had replaced his small car with a used Cadillac and took us all, including Phil, to Miami to welcome my aunt and her family. My grandmother, as always, refused to go.

My mother could hardly contain herself during the trip.

"My little sister. At last! Thank you, God," she kept saying as my father drove to Miami on I-75. My father smiled at first, but after a while, he took out a cigarette and began to smoke. He looked nervous. I wondered if it was Aunt Berta's arrival or the reason for which he'd left Miami that had him on edge.

"Rio, can you open the window a little?" Mother said. He complied.

After three or four puffs, he closed the window and put out his cigarette; however, he started to scratch his hand repeatedly, like he did when he was nervous.

Phil and I held hands most of the trip, something we could do in my father's presence. Anything else, he considered disrespectful. Throughout the trip, we engaged in small talk. Phil talked about his disc-jockey gigs, the great mixes he could do, the reactions from people at the parties. I saw my father roll his eyes and shake his head, but luckily Phil did not see him.

Phil told me he asked for extra hours at the grocery store where he worked, so he could save more money. My father occasionally observed him through the rearview mirror, while I glanced at my father.

When we arrived in Miami, Father took us to a popular pizza place called "El Rey de la Pizza" and ordered a medium with *chorizo* to share and *guarapo* to wash it down. This meal was not intended to be our lunch, only a snack to hold us over until my aunt arrived. The smell of melted cheese and fresh tomato sauce made my stomach growl as I anxiously awaited.

"This is the real Cuban pizza," he said. "Nothing better!"

The arrival of the food validated his words. I had never eaten a pizza as crispy, cheesy, and tasty as that one, not even at the Sorrento Pizzeria, my favorite pizzeria back in Havana.

My father looked around the table with pride as we ate and praised the pizza. He then glanced at my mother, patted her arm, and smiled.

Before we left the restaurant to continue our drive, my father gave the waitress a tip that made her beam with happiness and caused my mother to shake her head.

Later, as our car approached Miami International Airport, my mother started to weep. "I cannot believe I'm going to see my sister again after so long," she said.

"Laura," my father replied. "You need to calm down. You know how much your blood pressure goes up when you get like this. The important thing is that she is almost here. Take a deep breath."

While focused on the road, he reached for her arm and rubbed it a few strokes. She nodded, wiped her face, and inhaled deeply.

Mother's anticipation grew once we arrived at Miami International, as families gathered to welcome their loved ones.

"Is that their plane?" Mom would ask each time a group of people made their appearance.

Anxiously, Mom scanned every face, until her eyes became fixed on one.

"Berta?" she yelled and began to wave. "Berta! I'm here! Oh my God, I cannot believe it. Berta! My little sister!"

My aunt nervously looked in the direction from where the voice was coming and when their eyes met, both sisters ran towards each other and embraced.

"My sister. I cannot believe you are here!" my mother said, her voice cracking. "When I left Cuba, I was afraid I would never see you again!"

My aunt did not respond, but the way she held my mother's gaze, her face reddened, her eyes moist—and the long, heartfelt embrace she gave her sister said it all.

They brought up the emotions of those who saw them. Happiness poured from them, like water from a spring. The love they felt for each other was infectious, bringing smiles mixed with tears to the witnesses of their encounter.

Aunt Berta and Uncle Antonio looked thinner and older than I remembered them, and their two girls, now six and eight, had grown so much. My aunt and uncle wore black slacks and blue tops and the girls, pink dresses.

I shyly looked at my uncle not knowing what to do. He had been the only father I had known when I lived in

Cuba, but we never showed affection towards each other. Like my father, he concealed his emotions. Yet, he did not need to tell me he loved me to reveal what was in his heart. The way he helped me with homework and explained complex subjects, the times he sat with me to play as I was growing up, and the reluctant tear that escaped his eyes when he first saw us at Miami International unveiled what he felt.

I approached Uncle Antonio and embraced his tall, skinny body.

"Hey, Tania!" he said awkwardly as if he had seen me the day before, and instead of embracing me, he patted me on my back. I smiled.

"Good to see you, Uncle Antonio."

Moments later, while I was greeting Aunt Berta, I noticed that Phil was not by my side, but had stayed a few steps behind. I signaled him to come over, and he approached me timidly.

"Aunt Berta," I said in Spanish. "This is my boyfriend, Phil."

She looked at Phil and her eyebrows rose a notch.

"Boyfriend?" she said. "You are too young for boyfriends!"

"But I am almost eighteen!"

My aunt rolled her eyes and shook her head.

"These kids want to grow up too fast," she said. "Come over here, Phil. Give Aunt Berta a hug."

Phil smiled nervously and gave her a careful embrace.

"Look how big you are!" she said. "And all of you have gained a few pounds since you left! Especially you, Tania."

"Antonio! Antonio!" a female voice yelled.

We all looked in the direction from where the voice was coming from and saw three or four people approaching us, all wearing smiles. My uncle Antonio noticed his sister among the group and ran towards her. Another emotional encounter. She had left Cuba in the 1960s, and they were now meeting again, over twenty years later.

After spending some time at the airport, the entire group went to Versailles, a popular restaurant in Miami. Antonio's family insisted in paying for everyone. It was a delicious meal consisting of black beans, rice, *picadillo,* plantains, and smiles. During our feast, we learned that my aunt and her family would stay in Miami. Antonio's family had rented a house that accommodated the couple and their daughters. I was a little disappointed that they were not coming to Tampa with us, but my mother explained later that my uncle's family had been in the United States much longer than we had and were in a better position to help them.

That night, after we said goodbye to Aunt Berta and Uncle Antonio, we drove back to Tampa. My mother could not wait to see her sister again.

***

A couple of days after my aunt's arrival, Grandma asked me to go outside with her, and we sat under the oak tree.

"Last night, I tried to kill myself," she said casually.

"Grandma! That is not funny," I said, bringing my hand to my chest. "You should not talk like that."

"You see this mark?" she said, pointing at her arm. "I tried to cut my arm, but the knife was not sharp enough."

"Grandma, please don't say these things. You are scaring me. Our priest said that people who do that will go to hell."

"Ah! What does the priest know about heaven and hell," she said dismissively. "Anyhow, I need you to do me a favor."

"What is it?"

"Remember, long time ago, when I asked you to write a poem for me?"

"I do remember," I said.

"I will tell you how I feel now, so you can write about it. It's time."

"What do you mean?"

"Don't mind me. Just listen."

I listened to her attentively.

"I miss my sister," she said grabbing my hands between hers. "I miss her family, my little home where, even if I did not have much, I had my dignity and controlled my life. Here, under someone else's roof, someone else's rules, I feel invisible. No one cares about what I say. I am always the intruder. And look at me!"

She touched her arms and face and her expression transformed with disgust.

"What do you mean?"

"I was a beautiful, vibrant woman. A woman that, after being a widow at a young age and losing her first son, managed to pick up the pieces and build a little fortune when it was not common for women to buy and rent apartments. That was something only men did back then. Where is that woman now? And where is the man I loved for so many years? Rio doesn't understand that when he took me out of Cuba, he ripped my heart in two."

Her eyes glistened with tears. I hugged her.

"Don't be sad, Grandma. You have your son and grandchildren here."

She shook her head.

"I'm like a piece of old, useless furniture that someone keeps in a dark room. That is how I feel. I need you to write about it. It is important for me."

"I will. I promise," I said.

The next day, we met again, and I reluctantly showed her the gloomy poem. She read the pages quietly, and when she was done, she raised her head slowly and our eyes met. I will never forget the intensity of that look.

"Thank you," she said, and hugged me. "Now that everyone will know how I feel, I can die in peace."

"Why do you mean?" I asked.

She smiled. "Don't worry about me. I'm old, and old people say silly things. You focus on your school and make us proud. And one more thing, never forget how much I love you."

It was not until the next day that I understood her words.

My father and I had just returned from the grocery store, when we noticed my sister in front of the house. She seemed alarmed.

"Dad, hurry! Something is wrong," she said, waving us in her direction repeatedly, as if she were directing traffic.

"What do you mean?" he asked. We exited the car quickly and rushed to my sister.

She placed her hand on her chest and breathed heavily.

"It's Grandma, Dad!" she said, and broke into tears.

"What happed?" asked my father.

"She went into the bathroom. Then, I heard a popping noise. I started calling her name, and she is not answering. I think she did something, but I am afraid to open the door."

Chills went through my body as I recalled my conversation with her.

"Dad, you stay here. I'll go inside," I said.

I did not know why my father did not insist he should be the one to go, but the despair in his eyes conveyed his preoccupation.

Chapter 11 - Goodbye

I trembled when I entered the house. Everything was eerily quiet.

"Grandma. It's me, Tania. Are you okay?"

No answer. I knocked on the bathroom door. Still no answer. I went into her bedroom and the bed was neatly made, her bedspread of tiny pink flowers without a wrinkle. The shade was up and the morning sun entered through the closed window. I returned to the bathroom and stood in front of the door. I knocked gently.

"Grandma, I am coming in."

I opened the door slowly, listening to the squeaking noise of the hinges. I brought my hand to my mouth when I saw her legs, then the rest of her body, resting in a pool of blood. I saw a gun by her side, her hand on her chest. My body trembled and my eyes filled with tears.

"Why Grandma? Why?" I asked, my voice cracking. "Can you hear me?"

No answer. I was afraid to touch her and stayed frozen in place, in disbelief.

Moments later, I tried to compose myself and went outside, unsure of how to deliver the news to my father. He was walking in my direction when I exited the bathroom. I took a deep breath.

"Whatever you do, Dad, do not go in there," I said, shaking my head and quivering. "You do not want to see her like that."

"What happened?"

"She shot herself, Dad!" I said, trying to hold the tears. "She's not responding. There's blood everywhere. Please sit down. I will call 911."

For a moment, my father became motionless, transfixed by astonishment and pain. Then, his amber eyes turned glassy and his lips quivered. He turned his head away from me, and I could hear his uneven breathing, his gasping for air. I tried to keep it together. I did not want him to see me cry.

"Operator?" I said in broken English. "We have an emergency. It's my grandmother. She shot herself. We live on LaSalle Street. Please hurry!"

I was too nervous to think. She asked for our full address, but I had a hard time remembering it. Finally, I blurted out the number. She asked me other questions I could not decipher, because by then, I was not actively listening, but dumbfounded, recreating what I had just seen in my mind.

"Please hurry," I said, and hung up.

My father stumbled and sat down on the sofa suddenly. He raised his arms and interlaced his fingers behind his neck. My sister sat next to him, sobbing, and embraced him.

"They're coming, Dad," I said somberly, but I could not stay near my father or say anything else. I turned around and headed for the backyard.

I sat on one of the chairs under the oak tree where my grandmother and I had conversed about Cuba and the life we left behind, and began to weep uncontrollably. All the conversations with my grandmother had led to this.

I did not know how long I sat under the oak tree. When I looked down, I noticed that Danny was lying down at my feet. I heard the ambulance arrive, but I could not stand. My legs felt heavy. After a while, I looked towards the front of the house and beyond the chain-link fence. I saw the paramedics rolling my grandmother away on a stretcher, her body covered by a white sheet. I hoped that they had found a pulse. I could not tell if her head was covered. But something told me that she would not return. Danny ran towards the fence when he saw the stretcher and barked at the men. When my grandmother's body disappeared into the ambulance, he remained silent, observing the paramedics. After they left, Danny returned to my side and sat near my feet quietly.

In that stretcher, the history of my grandmother and great-grandparents, my ties to Cuba, and our traditions rolled away.

We had no money for the funeral. We called our relatives, but not many were able to help, and we did the best we could with the little money we had. Grandma had a short, intimate service attended by a small group of friends. Cremation was a cheaper option than a burial, but the idea of cremating her horrified us. She had a bouquet of flowers that we purchased at a nearby flower shop, nothing fancy, and a couple of vases Phil's family and our Town and Country friends had sent. Grandma was buried at the least expensive cemetery we could find, the kind of place none of us would want to visit alone. Phil and his family accompanied us to the funeral home and to the cemetery where her body was laid to rest.

Later, we notified her sisters in Cuba by phone. My father could not speak to his aunts without breaking down, and Mother had to deliver the news. We could hear the screams from where we sat in the dining room, a few steps from the telephone, our eyes filling with tears.

My brother refused to sleep in Grandma's bedroom that night, and my sister and I were afraid to be in our rooms alone, thinking that her spirit still roamed the house. For the next couple of days, we all slept in my parents' bedroom. The first night after her burial, we heard a knock on the door. We *all* heard it! My father rushed out of the bedroom and checked the entire house. There was no one there.

My mother believed that Grandma's spirit was not resting, as she had died in such a violent manner. Despite my father's protests, my mother placed a full glass of water on top of the refrigerator and prayed for her soul to rest in peace.

We never heard knocks on the door again.

Chapter 12 - The Aftermath

After his mother's death, Rio became withdrawn. He smoked almost a pack a day and drank more heavily. In the evenings, he lay next to me in silence for long periods of time.

"I love you," I would tell him.

"Me too," he would respond mechanically, while his mind seemed far away. I did not know what to do.

One Saturday evening, as we watched television with the children, the telephone rang. Tania rushed to pick it up thinking it was Phil, but moments later, she joined us in the living room and announced:

"It's a call for Dad."

Rio swung his hand back dismissively.

"Ah! Probably a salesman," he said. To me, he added, "Can you see what they want, my love?" He stroked my hair.

We did not have a cordless telephone back then, so I got up, walked towards the dining room and picked up the handset.

"Hello," I said.

"Are you Laura, Rio's wife?" a female voice asked in Spanish.

"Yes. Do I know you?"

"You don't, but I feel I know you. Rio has talked so much about you through the years."

"I'm sorry," I said. "I don't know who you are, or how you know my husband. Who gave you this number?"

"I can sense your apprehension in your voice, but don't worry. Rio told me that the moment his family arrived in the United States, we would never see each other again. I just wanted to see how he was doing. As to where I obtained your number, your sister gave it to me when I visited Cuba over a year ago. But I was not prepared to call back then."

"Did you and my husband . . .?" I asked.

She took a deep breath.

"Look. We were very good friends, and the past is the past. You have nothing to worry about. True. I loved your husband very much. I still do. He is the most amazing man I have ever known, but he always told me how important you and his children were to him, and I understood it very clearly. He told me so much about you that I feel like I know you. You are a very lucky woman."

I remained silent, not knowing what to say.

"Listen. I don't want to inconvenience you any longer. Tell him that Aurora called to see how he was doing. Something told me that he was not doing well, but I see that is not the case," she said.

"His mother just passed away," I said, only to regret it as those words left my mouth.

"Oh no! I am so sorry. Please give him my condolences. I can only imagine how he feels." She paused for a moment and took a deep breath. "Look, I won't take any more of your time. I hope you and Rio have a happy life."

After I hung up, I was not sure how to react. So many thoughts rushed through my head, and I felt vulnerable. Not having enough time to think about how to address the issue, I returned to the living room and sat next to Rio quietly.

"Who was it?" he asked, his eyes glued to the television.

"Aurora just called," I said with a serious expression.

"Who?"

"You know exactly who," I said in a monotone voice, my eyes glued on the television.

He turned his head towards me.

"How did she get this number?" he asked.

"She went to Cuba about a year ago and got it from my sister," I said, then, turning to him, I added: "Is this the reason you have been so quiet and distant all these days?"

Rio shook his head. "That's not it," he said. "Let's go to our bedroom and talk there."

We walked quietly to our bedroom, closed the door, and sat on the bed. I felt sad and betrayed and those feelings reflected in my expression.

"Did you sleep with this woman?" I asked.

Rio breathed deeply and grabbed my hands.

"I don't want to hurt you by answering that question."

"Are you still seeing her?"

"No, you have it all wrong," he said.

"Do I? I have been so concerned about your sadness after the loss of your mother. I kept asking myself how to help you get out of the emptiness she left and not finding the answer, but all along, it was not your mother, but another woman?"

I shook my head.

"My behavior has nothing to do with her," he said. "I have not seen that woman for a long time. I made it very clear to her that after my wife and my children came, my previous life would end. Only my family mattered. I have been true to that promise."

My eyes filled with tears.

"For almost twelve years I waited for you. There was never anyone else in my life," I said.

He took a deep breath.

"We have had this conversation before. I was alone in a strange country. You had the children and your family. I felt lonely."

"Is she the reason why you were distant?"

Rio shook his head. "No," he said.

"Then why?"

"I'd rather not talk about it," he said, looking away.

"I need to now, Rio, especially now."

He remained silent for a moment. Finally, he inhaled deeply and exhaled.

"Fine," he said. "I think you're right. I'm not used to telling others what I think, not anymore. I have to get used to being your husband again. So here is what has kept me quiet all these days. Since my mother left me at the orphanage when I was nine, after my father and my brother died, and especially after she refused to get me out of that damned place, I've been angry. I stopped loving her. When she took her life, I felt guilty. I blamed myself. If I had only been a man and stopped letting my stupid feelings get in the way. She was my mother, God damn it! What kind of person does not love his mother? I felt then that I did not deserve having a family." His lips quivered as he looked at me with misty eyes.

"Oh, Rio, my love. You *do* deserve your family and so much more. You may not be a perfect man, none of us are, but who else would have waited almost twelve years for their family? Only you, Rio. I knew that regardless of what you said about your mother, you had a special place for her in your heart."

Rio shook his head.

"I don't deserve you. I never have."

"I want no one else, Rio. Just you," I said, caressing his face.

He held me in his arms and kissed me. “I miss her,” he said, his voice cracking.

“I know, my love. I know.”

Chapter 13 - Pregnant

For months, Phil had been asking me to consider taking our relationship to another level.

"A man has needs," he would tell me.

"Fulfill them with someone else! I can't," I told him each time.

I may have been the only virgin in my senior year, but that was the way my mother had raised me, and he respected my decision and did not pressure me.

After we both completed high school, as we started to spend more time together between classes at the university, I realized that I would not able to continue to wait much longer.

We loved each other very much. That was clear. I had never been able to talk to anyone as I did to him. We spoke on the telephone for hours, and had a little competition before we said goodbye for the evening.

"I love you," I would say.

"No, I love *you*," Phil would respond.

And this would continue for some time until my father, tired of the back and forth, would tell me to hang up once and for all.

Phil was intelligent, thoughtful, and kind, and seemed to care for me deeply. My parents did not want us to get married, yet we wished more than anything to be together forever. I wrote many poems about Phil and read them to him when he visited. It was an old-fashion romance not seen in the 1980s, but things could not remain the way they were for much longer. And by the time we finally made love, after I had turned eighteen, we could not stay away from each other. Yet, I felt incredibly guilty and ashamed. How could I look my mother in the face again?

A couple of weeks after our first time, when my period did not come, I was worried. I waited a few more days thinking that the stress had caused a delay, but then, I began to notice changes.

"There is a place by the university that gives free pregnancy tests," Phil suggested. "Let's go there first to make sure."

Sometime later, as we sat in the waiting room of an abortion clinic near the University of South Florida, I could feel my hands getting cold and clammy from the anticipation. Finally, a nurse approached us, and her words jolted my body like lightning.

"You're pregnant," she said, after she sat next to me.

I looked into Phil's black eyes, beyond the thick lenses he wore in 1983. He remained speechless. The way the nurse examined our confused and fearful faces made me realize she had witnessed similar reactions many times before, and confirmation of this came moments later:

"You have options, you know," she said.

Options? She clearly did not know my father, the first face I pictured in my mind when she delivered the news.

She went on to describe the abortion procedure. Her depiction horrified me more than the thought of having to confront my father. And the strangest thing occurred as I touched my belly and my maternal instincts awoke.

"Abortion?" I asked. "I could never kill my own child! I couldn't."

I glanced at Phillip, and my eyes filled with tears. He seemed frozen in place.

"Oh my God. My father is going to kill me when I tell him!" I said. "We have to go."

I grabbed Phil by his arm and left the nurse standing with my chart in her hand. When we stepped outside the clinic, Phil noticed a public telephone booth.

"I need to speak to my mother," he said.

I wanted the earth to swallow me at that moment.

"My father," I said, with my voice cracking. "Oh my God. What have I done? How can I tell him this? He will kill both of us!"

Phil placed his hands behind his head. He knew my father carried a .45-caliber gun with him everywhere he went. The way my father scanned his surroundings when we went out made Phil think he was crazy.

"I need to speak to my mother," he repeated.

I stayed a couple of feet away from him, caressing my belly and crying.

He pressed the numbers. After a few moments, shaky words came out of his mouth.

"Mom," he said. "We have a problem. Tania is pregnant."

I could not tell what was happening on the other end of the line, no matter how hard I tried to read his face. The call went on for a while, but Phil hardly said anything.

"She wants to talk to you," he said.

His mother spoke softly, in a reassuring manner.

"The two of you can move into my house. Where two can eat, three or four can eat. We are not rich, but we will share what we have with you and the baby."

Her words and the kindness in her voice felt comforting, but then I recalled my father's words.

"If anyone ever messes with my family," he had said, touching his gun, "they will have to deal with me."

The seriousness in his eyes had led me believe he was not bluffing.

I returned the handset to Phil. All I could hear after that was "Okay . . . okay . . . okay."

When the conversation ended, we stood there looking into each other's eyes. I knew what he was thinking.

"I can never have an abortion. I'm sorry. I could not," I said.

He embraced me.

"Don't worry," he said. "I'll do whatever I need to do."

He opened the passenger door of his 1974 Plymouth Duster for me and drove me back to USF.

I attended classes for the rest of the day, but could not concentrate. Later, when my father picked me up, I could hardly speak.

"Did you have a good day?" he said, with a big smile.

"Yes," I answered unconvincingly, staring at the dashboard.

Maintaining his eyes on the road, he said, "I have a surprise when we get home. I made my special pizza. Took me hours to make it."

"Thank you, Dad," I said, feeling deeply ashamed.

It saddened me the way he tried so hard to make his children happy, his insistence on doing everything he could to make up for the lost years. And now, I was about to break his heart.

Later that evening, after dinner, after we sat on the lower level of our bunk beds, I shared the news with my sixteen-year-old sister. We were both wearing the same nightgowns made with a colorful-striped cotton-blend fabric. Our hair was down. When I was finished, she opened her mouth wide and covered it with her hand. Moments later, she shook her head and said:

"Dad is going to kill you!"

She wanted details, but I did not volunteer any.

"I am eighteen years old. I told Mom we wanted to get married. She thought I was kidding," I said.

"I don't think he cares if you are eighteen or thirty. He's still going to kill you."

I took a deep breath and prepared for bed silently.

"Can I see your belly?" she asked.

I raised my nightgown and showed her. She noticed a small bump.

"Oh my God! You are *so* pregnant!" she said looking at me. Then, touching my belly, she added, "Hello, little baby. I'm your aunt, Lynette. Your mom is in so much trouble."

"I'm scared," I said. "I don't think I will leave my bedroom tonight."

"I won't either," said my sister, embracing me.

She turned on the radio and began to dance to Salsa music, while I removed my journal from the bag I took to school. I needed to write. That was the only way I could relax. As I was thinking about what to write, I noticed the happiness that emanated from my sister when she danced, the way music transported her and made her contort her body. She was a great dancer, and even though she told me time and time again how much she wished she had my brain, I wished I had just a little of her happiness.

Around eight that evening, my mother came into our room. By that time, we were both sitting on the bottom bed talking about what to do. When we saw our mother, we stopped talking. My sister got up, and as she was about to climb to the second level, our eyes met briefly.

"Ready for bed, or do you want to watch some television with your father and me?" our mother asked, while she tucked her blond, shoulder-length hair behind her ear.

I shook my head, while my sister raised her eyebrows and tapped her fingers together nervously.

"Is everything okay?" my mother asked.

I swallowed, concerned she could see through the fear etched on my face.

"Mom . . . there is something I have to tell you," I said. "Please sit next to me."

She hesitated and then complied, while my sister watched us, like a statute with mechanical eyes moving from side to side as my mother and I talked.

"You know that Phil and I love each other," I said as I played with my fingers and thought about my next words. "You remember the day he told you he wanted to marry me, but you thought we are too young and should finish school first."

"Of course you are too young, and he is not mature enough to marry anyone."

Feeling a little dizzy, I took a deep breath. I had to let her know. I could not keep it to myself any longer. I lifted my head and looked into my mother's eyes with shame.

"Mom, I'm pregnant."

The moment I said those words, my mother's face turned red like one of the stripes on my nightgown.

"You what?" she asked. "Did I hear what I thought I heard?"

I nodded.

She got up, lifted her arms, and interlaced her fingers over her head.

"Do you understand what you have done?" she asked. She looked up for a moment and then paced nervously around the room.

"Oh my God! I cannot believe this. Tell me this is not true."

I started to weep.

"I am so sorry, Mom," I said, placing my hand on her shoulder.

She jerked away, speechless at first, as anger and disappointment took hold of her expression.

"Do you know how much I sacrificed myself to reunite our family with your father in the United States?" she raged. "I wanted you to have the opportunities you would never have in Cuba. I wanted to give you a united family. I put my life on hold for my children, gave you everything I had, and *this* is how you repay me?"

She massaged her temples with her fingers. "I have to tell your father," she said.

"No, Mom please," I begged. "He will kill me."

She took a deep breath.

"This is not something I can hide. I never thought that you, out of all my children, would do this to me. You have disappointed me so much."

She looked at me one last time, shook her head, and stormed out of the room.

"What do I do now?" I asked Lynette.

She scratched her head.

"Oh my God, Tania. You're *so* dead."

We turned off the lights to our bedroom, locked the door, and listened quietly. We could hear loud voices, but could not decipher the words. The voices moved to the yard, right outside my window. I slightly moved the shades to take a look.

What I saw terrified me. My father waved his gun in the air.

"I will kill him. I swear I will!" he yelled.

I don't know why, but I believed he meant every word.

"Lynette," I whispered. "I have to go!"

"What do you mean?"

"I have to go!"

I unlocked the door and rushed out my bedroom wearing my nightgown and no shoes. I could still hear my father's voice yelling from the yard. I ran in the opposite direction towards the corner, not knowing where I was going, but I had to get as far away from our house as I could. A tear trickled down my cheek and my legs trembled.

As I ran, I remembered an elderly woman who lived about a block away and always said hello when we passed by. I decided to go there. She seemed like someone I could trust.

I knocked on her door frantically. At last, the light in front of the house turned on and moments later, she opened.

With my voice cracking, I asked in Spanish, "Can I use your phone?"

The woman had white hair combed back and into a bun. She wore a pink night robe, glasses, and now, under the glow of the yellow light, her faced seemed more wrinkled than I recalled.

"Is everything ok?" she asked, also in Spanish.

I shook my head. "I have an emergency and need to use your phone to call my boyfriend!" I said—then looking down and placing my hands across my belly, I added, "My father just found out I am pregnant. He's in the backyard with a gun. He wants to kill my boyfriend. I am so scared!"

As soon as I said those words, the nice woman quickly opened her door to let me in. She looked on either side of her door before closing it, then turned to me.

"I'm so sorry to hear he reacted like that. Please make yourself comfortable," she said. "The phone is on the end table. Take a deep breath and calm down. I will bring you a glass of water. By the way, my name is Beverly, and you?"

"Tania."

"Don't worry, Tania. Your father is nervous, but he will come to his senses," she said, patting me on my back.

"You don't know my father," I said, shaking my head.

She smiled like a grandmother, her years of wisdom emanating from her kind eyes.

"I'll be right back, sweetheart. Make your phone call," she said, and disappeared into the back of the house.

I walked a couple of steps on the white tile floor and picked up the handset noticing the small, but well-organized living room: a beige upholstered sofa and loveseat, a dark oval wooden table, adorned by a silver vase, and matching square end tables with lit lamps. My hands trembled as I pressed the digits. Finally, on the other end, I heard Dalia, Phil's mother.

"Can I talk to Phil?" I said. "It's urgent!"

"Who is this?"

"Tania."

"Is everything okay?" she asked.

"No, not really," I said. "I need to speak to Phil. It is very important."

"He's here. I'll give him the phone."

I took a deep breath.

"Tania, are you okay?"

"I need you to come get me!" I said, trying to hold back the tears. "I am at a neighbor's house, to the east of mine, about a block from where live. I ran away."

"What happened?" he asked.

"My dad lost his temper when he heard about my pregnancy. He took out a gun and . . ."

Phil did not wait for my next words. I heard a noise on the other side of the telephone, followed by undecipherable yelling. I called his name, but he did not answer. Moments later, his mother picked up the handset.

"Tania, Phil is coming for you," she said. "He looked as if he had gone crazy and said horrible things that I won't repeat. Then he ran out of the house. I hope he doesn't do anything he regrets."

"What did he say?" I asked.

"Don't worry about it. He was nervous because he cares for you very much."

"What am I going to do now?" I asked. "I can't go back home!"

"He's bringing you here, and you can share his room. We'll figure it out. Don't worry. You need to stay calm."

I put down the handset and told Beverly that Phil was on his way. After I described his car to her, she suggested I stay inside while she waited on the porch. She left me in the dimly lit living room, afraid that at any time my father would storm through the front door with the gun.

I sat on the sofa, but I could not stay still. My hands were clammy and cold and my right leg kept shaking. Time went by slowly after that. I could hear the ticking of the wall clock getting louder and louder.

Feeling ashamed and guilty, I thought about the priest and the nuns at St. Joseph's Church. I needed to confess my sins to God, and hoped he would forgive me. I started to pray for my parents, for the baby I was carrying, and for Phil.

After a long while, the sound of screeching brakes made me jump out of my seat. Moments later the door opened, and Phil rushed in, followed by Beverly. He hurried towards me and held me tightly around my waist.

"Are you okay?" he asked. "Did he hit you?"

I shook my head.

"No, no," I said. "I ran out when I saw him so upset."

"I don't want you to go back," he said, looking into my eyes. "You're coming with me."

Beverly stood by the front door watching us, Phil's back towards her. I saw her turn to look at a black-and-white wedding picture on the wall. She pressed her lips together and looked down.

"Phil," I said. "This is Beverly. She was very kind to allow me to use her telephone and stay here until you came."

Phil and I thanked her, gave her a hug, and left.

Once in the car, the mere mention of my father angered Phil so much that he started to drive very fast, spinning the wheels. I got scared and decided not to mention him again.

The porch of his house on Clifton Street had the lights on when we arrived. Dalia sat outside on a rocking chair with one of her twins on her lap.

Phil asked the six-year-old twin boys to go to the family room to watch television, so the adults could speak.

"Tell me what happened, sweetheart," asked Dalia as she sat next to me on the long sectional and patted my back, her husband, Jose, next to her.

I was in the middle of my explanation when the telephone rang. Phil and I exchanged glances, while Dalia walked to the dining room, adjacent to the room where we sat, and picked it up.

"Hello," she said, and remained silent for a while.

"Yes, Tania is here," Dalia added moments later. She turned her head towards me, and covering the mouthpiece with one hand, she whispered: "It's your mom."

We all remained silent while Dalia and my mother spoke. Phil held my hand and looked at his mother, as if trying to decipher what she was hearing.

"Don't worry, Laura," Dalia said after another long silence. "They will get married. Do you want to speak to your daughter?"

I glanced at Phil's mother and swallowed when she offered me the handset. My hands turned cold as I brought it to my ear.

"Yes, Mom?" I asked.

"Do you have any idea who called the police on your father?" she asked.

"The police?" I asked, turning to Phil. Feeling light-headed, I pulled a chair from the dining room and sat down. "I swear it was not me."

"They came to our house and confiscated your father's gun," she explained. "They also took him into custody."

"Oh my God!" I said on the verge of tears. Phil came over to my side and placed his arm around me. "It wasn't me, Mom. Maybe a neighbor overheard him. I don't know what to say, other than I'm sorry. I never meant for any of this to happen."

She took a deep breath.

"What will the neighbors think? I am so embarrassed. Years of my life sacrificed for you, to bring you to this country, so you could make something with your life, and this is how you repay me? Is this what I deserve? How will I explain this to your brother and sister?"

I remained silent trying to hold back the tears, realizing nothing I could tell her would change how she felt.

"I have a lot on my mind, and now, I have to figure out how to bail your father out of jail," she said. "There is one last thing I must tell you. You need to marry that boy to save me further embarrassment. And do not sleep with him again until you do! Do I make myself clear?"

"Yes, Mom." I said. She remained silent for a moment.

"I don't know what your father will say when he returns home, but it will be best if you do not come here for a while." She inhaled deeply and then exhaled. "I can't talk to you anymore. This is upsetting me too much. Have a good life, Tania."

She hung up, leaving me empty and broken inside. Feeling the weight of my sin over my shoulders, I asked God for forgiveness.

Chapter 14 - Without My Daughter

Since Tania was a little girl, she showed tremendous promise paired with a commitment to excel. She would listen attentively to her uncle when he read complex books like *Territorial Expansion of the United States* and showed promise as a writer. A fortune teller once told me that Tania was destined for great things. If the same woman had not accurately predicted my mother's death, I would not have given any credence to her prediction. But my mother did die, in her fifties, shortly after the fortune teller told me she had seen her death in the cards.

My expectations of Tania made it so much more difficult to witness how she had thrown away her future.

After she left, the police came to our house, questioned Rio like a common criminal, and handcuffed him in front of my other children. I assumed one of our neighbors must have notified the authorities when they heard his threats.

Our Puerto Rican friends took me to the police station and helped me post bail. I explained to the officers that Rio posed no danger to his family. He had never been violent with us, but the alcohol and the sudden news had caused his reaction.

Chapter 14 - Without My Daughter

It was early morning by the time Rio returned home, sober, pale, and with a somber look on his face. He gathered the family in the dining room and announced:

"Tania has died for this family. I do not want anyone here to speak to her, or of her, or to see her. The moment she left this house, she stopped being my daughter!"

I crossed my arms and looked at him wide-eyed. "But Rio, you cannot ask me to forget about my daughter!" I protested.

"Dad, Tania is my sister," Lynette said. "She will always be my sister."

Rio slammed the table. "I am sick and tired of everyone in this family arguing with me! Whoever does not like it, there is the door," he said, pointing to the front door. "Do I make myself clear?"

I was speechless and felt trapped. I considered leaving him that very second, but I thought about my other children who needed a stable home and their father.

"She is our baby girl," I tried to reason with him. "Just because she made a mistake, you cannot write her off. How many mistakes did we make when we were her age?"

He gave me a hard and angry stare.

"This conversation is over," he said. "I'm going to shower and get a few hours of sleep. I don't want anybody to bother me."

Rio walked away, while Lynette, Gustavo, and I looked at each other, dumbfounded.

"Can someone tell me what is going on?" said twelve-year-old Gustavo.

"You are a child," Lynette said. "This is an adult conversation, so stay out of it."

Gustavo gave Lynette a little push.

"Hey, do not push your sister," I said.

"Well," Gustavo said, turning to me. "Can you tell me what happened? Why did Tania leave? Where did she go?"

He turned the palms of his hands up and stared at me, wide-eyed.

"Your sister and Phil are getting married," I said.

He raised his eyebrows.

"Are we invited?" he said.

"No, we are not going. No one is," he said.

Gustavo shrank his eyebrows, a suspicious look etched on his face. Then, as if he had figured it out, he placed his hands on his head.

"Oh my God! No! She didn't!" he said.

"What are you talking about, you idiot?" Lynette asked.

"Tania is pregnant!" he said. "She is in so much trouble."

He started to laugh.

"What are you laughing at?" Lynette said, and pushed him.

"The two of you stop it this very second! Please go to your room. You heard your father. He needs to rest." Then, turning to Gustavo, I added, "Everything that happens in this house, stays here. You hear me?"

"What's the big deal, Mom?" he asked. "Times have changed. We're not in Cuba anymore. I think it's funny. Me, an uncle at age twelve."

"It is *not* funny! Tania is smart. She had a full scholarship to the University of South Florida, and now she has ruined her life. That is no laughing matter, and we are not talking about this anymore. Both of you, go study, now!"

I pointed towards the back of the house.

"I am not going to stop talking to my sister, Mom," Lynette said as she walked away.

"I can't wait to tell my friends!" said Gustavo.

“You are not telling anyone, you hear?” I said grabbing him by his ear.

“Mom, you’re hurting me! Stop!”

“Are you going to tell anyone?”

“No, I’m not! Just kidding. Let go of my ear!”

I let him go.

“Everyone in this house is crazy,” he said rubbing his ear and walking away.

When my children disappeared in the back of the house, I looked around the room. On top of a cabinet, I noticed Tania’s typewriter and some paper. I already missed her. I had to do something to make her understand that no matter what, she still had me. I could not simply abandon her when she needed me the most.

Chapter 15 - The Arrival

On the tenth of October, on Columbus Day, Phil and I went to downtown to get married, but the courts were closed that day. When my mother learned that a day after moving in with my fiancé, I remained a single woman, she slammed the telephone on me. On the eleventh, we returned to the courts.

"Where are your witnesses?" asked the judge, a man late in his fifties with a silver beard and glasses.

I did not understand his question. Three years after arriving to the United States, I was still learning English.

"We don't have any witnesses," said Phil.

"What about the rings?" he asked.

"Tania has an engagement ring. I was not able to buy her a wedding ring, and she cannot afford to buy me one either."

The judge took a deep breath, shook his head, and said, "Fine, we'll figure it out. Let me get my secretary to serve as a witness."

Moments later, the ceremony started. When the judge asked us to say our wedding vows, he turned to Phil first. "Repeat after me," he said.

Phil repeated perfectly what he said. When it was my turn, I froze.

"I don't understand what he's saying!" I told Phil in Spanish. "Do I have to say anything?"

Phil translated what I had said to the judge.

"Either you repeat these words, or I cannot marry you!" he said.

Phil placed his arm on my shoulder.

"Come on, you can say it. Even if you make a mistake, who cares? It's just us. Please repeat it. You don't want to tell your mom that we are still not married."

I shook my head. The judge read me the words again.

"I, Tania Valdes, take you, Phil Mendez, for my lawful husband," the judge said.

I asked him to repeat himself several times and to speak slowly. With significant difficulty, and not understanding half of what I was committing to, Phil and I were legally married.

Our decision would complicate our lives more than we ever thought possible. The rollercoaster ride was just starting.

Reality hit quickly. I had to work full time in order to make the money I needed for the baby, for a place of our own, and for a car for me. It was not possible to go to work without a car, and I could not continue to depend on Phil's parents forever. Soon, I realized it was not feasible to attend the university full time, and I had no choice but to abandon my full scholarship at the University of South Florida, a move I would later regret.

I started to work full time at a nearby Winn Dixie, but the money I was making was not enough. While working there, I met a young girl who suggested a way to cut down my costs:

"You can always give your baby up for adoption," she said. "That's what I did."

I looked at her in confusion. "You gave up your baby?" I said.

"Yes, her new parents will have to tell her about me when she is eighteen. They are well-off and can give her what I can't."

The thought of giving up my child horrified me. "I could never do that," I said.

We were outside the store on break. The young woman took out a cigarette and began to smoke.

"It wasn't easy," she said and took a puff.

"I have to find another way," I said.

We talked to various relatives about our situation, and one of them suggested that the military would be a viable alternative for Phil. But I did not want to be away from him, and neither did his mother. Still, Phil felt that he needed to do something to be ready for his new family and decided to sign up for the Air Force.

He trained hard to get ready for basic training, aided by one of our relatives who had over twenty years of service in the Army. Phil began to look even more handsome than before, muscular arms, tight abdomen, but the more I thought about being away from him, the more difficult it became.

"I don't want you to go," I said as we lay in bed one evening. "I'm going to miss you too much. My mom spent years away from my father, and I don't want that to happen to us."

He held me in his arms.

"I don't want to be away from you either, but our life can be better if I go. We need our own place."

"I know, but you are the only person I have left. I have no one else."

He kissed me passionately, a kiss wet with my tears.

As the time of his departure approached, we could not stay away from each other. We stayed up late every night talking about our plans, the cute house we were going to buy, and the name of our son or daughter.

Chapter 15 - The Arrival

When the dreaded day arrived, I woke up early and did not say much to anyone. My mother-in-law served us breakfast, *café con leche,* toast with butter, and eggs, but I hardly touched mine. My father-in-law insisted I eat everything on my plate, then ended up eating what I left. When he lived in Cuba, he had learned what it was like to go to bed without eating, and did not want to see good food go to waste.

We left Phil's house on Clifton Street, and his mom drove us to the processing center in West Tampa. Dalia and I stayed outside and waited. Later, as his bus departed, and we waved goodbye to him, Dalia started to weep and I held back tears. Phil saw us, waved, placed his fingers on his lips, and threw us a kiss.

As soon as I had an address for Phil, we began to exchange letters. He had been sent to the Lackland Air Force Base in San Antonio, Texas. By then, the invasion of Grenada had started, and I was fearful that at the end of the six-week basic-training period, he would be deployed there. Ronald Reagan's presidency had started in 1981, and now, over two years later, not only had he invaded Grenada in the Caribbean, he had begun a large military exercise in Europe that caused the deployment of over 16,000 U.S. troops.

The world was changing too rapidly, and I feared for Phil's safety. As hard as I was taking his departure, his mother took it even worse. Her blood pressure started to spike frequently, causing dizzy spells. Phil was everything to her. Her English was not good. He helped her translate important documents, and had been her shoulder to cry on during the years she was separated from her parents. They had stayed in Cuba when she left in 1968.

His mother and I wrote many letters to Phil, telling him how much we missed him. Meanwhile, other more powerful aspects of his life were making him and his superiors realize that the military was not for Phil.

When his superior officer, dressed in military attire, began to give him orders, it did not take long for the buried images of Cuban military men taking his father away by force to emerge. Phil saw those men in his superior officer, and their relationship exploded. Each time his commander demanded his respect in a rough style, Phil would grow more resentful of him, leading at first to an exchange of profane phrases between them, and finally to a physical altercation. Less than three weeks into the training, after long discussions and evaluations, Phil received a general discharge from the military.

When he returned home, he underwent a long period of depression.

"We'll find another way," I would tell him when I found him staring at the floor for long periods of time. He'd look at me through his thick lenses, shake his head, and say: "You deserve better."

"You are all I need. I didn't marry you for what you own, but who you are. You are a good man, and that is all I care about."

But his frustration grew as he saw my belly getting bigger, and we found ourselves still living at his parents' house, him working at the Montgomery Ward warehouse, off Waters Avenue, and me working as a cashier at Winn Dixie.

I did not see my parents that Christmas. Phil and I spent a quiet Christmas Eve with his parents and his twin brothers. I missed my parents, my siblings, and Danny. After dinner, I excused myself and went to my room to cry, while caressing my belly. I asked myself, *what future awaits the little baby I carry inside me?*

Phil and I were almost nineteen and we did not know anything about raising children. Perhaps my mother's assertion that we had a lot of growing up to do and had ruined our lives was an accurate reflection of our reality. And now, I thought, how would we get out of this hole?

Our desperation rose each day. In February, when I was seven months pregnant, Dalia and I saw a sign on the road advertising an inexpensive house for sale. It required only $1,500 down and payments that Phil and I could afford. We wanted to surprise Phil and scheduled an appointment. That day, I learned something new about my new country. As nice as people were in the United States, there were always those preying on the ignorant without any regard for the damage they caused. We paid a man $1,500 in cash and never saw that money again. He simply disappeared. Later, when we reported it to the authorities, I learned he had done this to multiple families in the Tampa area, and even though he was apprehended a few years later, we never recovered the money.

I had always believed that every experience in my life had a reason for being. From that experience I learned that I needed to do something so no one could take advantage of me again. I just did not know what, not with a baby on the way.

My mother and I began to communicate almost daily. She would call me from work during her breaks, when I was not scheduled to work at Winn Dixie, and I found comfort in her words. She would tell me that not all was lost. "After the baby is born, you should go back to college," she said. "You're a smart woman, and I believe in you."

The baby came a few days late. The night before, Phil and I went to bed about eleven, and in the middle of the night, copious amounts of liquid—at the time, I was not sure what it was—began to pour from me. I had never seen Phil so nervous before. He slipped into a pair of jeans and an old shirt and woke up everyone in the house.

"What do I do? What do I do?" he asked his mother, not knowing what all the liquid on the floor of our bathroom was.

His mother smiled. "It's nothing to worry about. Her water broke. You will be a dad soon. Just take her to the hospital. Your dad and I will join you a little later."

I took a quick shower, and we rushed out of the house. It took Phil fifteen minutes longer than normal to make it to Tampa General Hospital. As often as we had been there in the past, he simply kept going in circles and could not find the bridge to Davis Island.

My mother-in-law called my parents to deliver the news. Mom took off from work that day and asked my in-laws to pick her up on their way to the hospital. Lynette and Gustavo joined her. From the time they arrived, my mother, my siblings, and my in-laws drove the hospital staff crazy with all their questions and their insistence that they all needed to be in my room. At one point, one of the nurses kindly suggested that they go home to rest.

"We are a Cuban family," Phil explained. "When someone is having a baby, the whole family comes. It's our parents' first grandchild."

As my labor progressed, I became increasingly agitated, causing my blood pressure to rise. A few hours after my arrival at the hospital, a nurse ran in and checked one of the monitors. She seemed alarmed.

"Is everything okay?" I asked.

"For a moment, we could not see the baby's heartbeat," she said. "It's okay now. Don't worry. I will tell the doctor."

Moments later, she returned with a medication and injected it into my IV pump.

"What's wrong with the baby?" I cried.

"We need to induce labor," the nurse said.

Once the medication began to take effect, the pain grew in intensity. I had never experienced such an excruciating pain, as my uterine muscles tightened and relaxed. My body contorted wildly with each contraction–the pain pulling up and across my womb. I was exhausted. My blood pressure kept rising, making me think irrationally. *This is God's punishment for having extramarital sex with Phil. My mother was right. If I had never met him, I would not be in this situation. This is the last time I will ever get pregnant. Never again!*

With each thought, I became angrier and angrier, and I was no longer looking at Phil with the loving eyes of a wife. Little by little, through each contraction, I ripped off the wallpaper with my nails. Phil kept asking questions about the cables attached to me, but I had no patience. Finally, I had enough.

"This is all your fault!" I yelled at him as if I were possessed.

"What did I do?" he asked with a confused expression.

"You got me pregnant!"

At that time, two men wearing white gowns entered my room. One of them introduced the other: "This is a medical student. He is here to learn. Do you mind?"

When I did not answer, but stared at the physician with anger, my faced reddened, Phil responded:

"That's fine."

But there was something I did not like about this intern, at least, that was what my irrational mind told me then. Exhausted from the few hours of sleep, high blood pressure, and intense pain, I convinced myself that he was looking at my legs more than he needed to, and perception became reality.

"Out! I don't want you in this room. What am I? A science project?"

Phil's eyes opened wide. "I'm sorry," he said. "She is in a lot of pain."

"Don't worry. I understand," the intern said, and exited the room.

At last, when I was almost ten centimeters dilated, the nurses asked me to hold back. "Don't push yet! We have to take you to the delivery room!" one of them said.

After twenty-one hours in labor, I gave her an incredulous look. Don't push? I could not take the pain one more minute, and the stubborn person in me pushed as hard as I could. Later, after I arrived in the delivery room, I felt the cut from the episiotomy and the warmth of the blood rolling down. But as the little boy left my body to join the outside world, the pain was so much more than anything I had felt before, that it made the discomfort of the incision and the stitches that followed benign in comparison.

Later, when I was taken back to a room, Phil's eyes filled with tears when he saw his son for the first time. He held my hand, as if he had forgotten all my screams and accusations during the hours in labor. By then, most of the pain was gone and my blood pressure had normalized, allowing me to think more clearly.

He held his son in his arms for a while, examining every part of his tiny body.

"The grandparents must be anxious. You should go get them," I suggested.

Before Phil left the room, I added, "I'm sorry about all I said before. I love you."

He smiled. "I know," he said.

When Phil returned with several members of our family, the first person I noticed was my father. I had not seen him for months, and the emotion I felt was overwhelming.

"Dad! Come closer so you can look at your grandson," I said.

His eyes glistened when he examined the little baby. Phil Jr. echoed a blend of Phil and me. He had his father's dark hair and my wide face and fair skin, but he measured only eighteen inches and weighed a little over six pounds.

"Can I hold him?" he asked, scratching his hand.

I smiled. "Of course, Dad!"

My mother came to my father's side and kissed and hugged me.

"Look at him!" she said. "Our first grandson. He's so precious."

She caressed his face, and the baby's dark eyes opened and his red lips took the form of what appeared to be a smile.

"Look, Rio," she said. "He is smiling at us. He likes his grandparents. Is that right, little one, don't you love Grandma and Grandpa?"

Each of the other family members embraced me and took turns holding the baby.

At some point, my father went to the back of the room and told my mother, "I'm going outside for a moment. I'll be back."

My mother took the opportunity to approach me, while my mother-in-law, surrounded by Phil, my siblings, and Tom, held my son in her arms and talked to him with a baby voice.

"I missed you," my mother said, caressing my face. "Our home has not been the same without you."

"I missed you too, Mom," I said.

"You did?" she asked, as her eyebrows rose a notch.

I nodded, and she smiled.

"Your father is not a bad man," she added. "He wants the best for his family. Now that you have a baby, you will understand."

She embraced me, and unlike other times, I returned her embrace.

"Thank you," she whispered, her breathing uneven.

She sat by my side, and we engaged in small talk. After a while, Dalia returned the baby to me. We were all conversing happily, my sister and Phil joking around with each other, and the others laughing, when we noticed my father. He had entered the room holding a gift bag, flowers, and a teddy bear.

"The flowers are for you," he said. "The bear and the bag are for the baby."

I could not contain myself and started to weep.

"Thank you, Dad. I love you. I love you too, Mom. I missed you both," I said, my voice cracking. I extended my arms to my father, and we embraced.

Later, after the baby and I went home, my parents began to visit me almost daily, which gave me the opportunity to catch up with them. My parents wanted to sell the house on LaSalle Street.

"Too many memories," my mother said. "We started to get calls again, and your father is on edge. Besides, he has not been the same after the accident at the glass company. He is in constant pain. His boss agreed to settle with him for $10,000. We are going to open up a small glass company and list only the business telephone. Once your father works for himself, he can choose his hours."

Their search for another house that fit their requirements began.

My sister was attending the community college and had found a job working at a business office for a hospital. She met an older man who shared some of my father's interests, and they began to date.

My mother wanted someone else for my sister, but based on her experience with me, sometime later, when the man came to the house to ask for my sister's hand in marriage, she did not object.

The wedding plans delayed the house search, and shortly after she turned nineteen, Lynette had a modest wedding at a Protestant church. She was a beautiful bride. Her long, brown hair bounced in beautiful curls over her shoulders. Even my aunt and her family drove from Miami for the event. At last, my mother's dream of seeing a daughter in a white wedding dress had materialized. With the wedding behind them and one more person out of the home, my parents began to look for another house.

They found a house in Town and Country that had an unfinished shop in the back. My father used some of the workers' compensation money to furnish his shop with the equipment needed to establish a small glass company. He also purchased a used van to transport the glass.

His back still hurt, but having his own business gave him the luxury of working flexible hours and resting when the pain became too unbearable. The shop also allowed him to smoke and drink beer as he pleased, two habits that would eventually take a toll on his health.

My mother did most of the marketing. After a while, my father convinced her to quit her job at the hospital and organize the office and the appointments for their customers. She targeted all types of customers, from residential to catering firms.

Somehow, a local strip club heard about my parents' business and had them install a glass wall at its establishment. My mother thought she was going to die when she entered the place. She was not used to seeing nude or practically nude women walking around without a care in the world. She could not understand why the women worked at those places.

"Why don't they study at the university, with so many opportunities this country has to offer? Also, aren't they embarrassed to show their bodies to strangers?" she asked my father.

"Life is not as simple as you make it," my father said. "Some of those girls have been raped. Others don't have a support system and find themselves pregnant and with a child. Not everyone was born to be a professor, Laura.” Then he smiled and touched her cheek. “For the world to be the world, there has to be all kinds of people. Who are we to judge?”

My father always had a way to make my mother see life from a totally different perspective than her own. Educated by nuns, she had received a strict religious upbringing and had never been outside Cuba, while my father had been in a war, worked for a mobster, and lived in big cities like Madrid, New York, and Miami. Despite his weaknesses, she not only loved him, but pitied him, and this led her to be overly tolerant, especially when he had too much to drink.

Chapter 16 - Tracing the Path

I had to act behind the scenes to get Tania back on the right track, but I did not want her to notice it.

Tania had so much potential. Since she was a child, I noticed her curiosity for subjects that were above her comprehension. She knew all the letters and numbers by the time she turned three. Around age seven, she began to read chemistry books and memorized the names of chemical compounds. Her need to learn something new every day mesmerized me.

We lived in a country where everything was possible, and I wanted my children to take advantage of the blessings we had been afforded. I wanted them to achieve the American dream, even if it was too late for Rio and me.

When I heard people talk about the American dream, I noticed variations of what it meant for each person. For me, it signified a rewarding career, a solid financial future, little or no debt, and a place to call my own. It also meant staying together as a family and treating others with kindness and respect, no matter how far our aspirations took us. Some of my friends thought that I was aiming too high. To them, I would say, “Dream, and you shall achieve.”

Nothing was going to stop me from leading my children towards the future I envisioned for them. In Tania's case, I decided to work through her mother-in-law, whom she trusted, and eventually, through her employer.

Phil and Tania began to take computer classes in the evening at Leto High School, and once they completed their certificates, a job opened at a social club that provided medical benefits for the hospital where I worked. I spoke to the office manager and begged him to interview Tania.

Tania had never held an office job. She was twenty years old then, and not understanding business etiquette, showed up to the interview with her mother-in-law and the baby in her arms. My daughter was wearing a simple, polka-dot dress with ruffles that her father-in-law had bought for her, not professional attire by any means. The office manager asked her to leave the baby with Dalia during the interview.

He was a tall man who wore glasses and acted awkwardly, an accountant whose family had emigrated from Spain. After Tania completed a math test he gave her, he reviewed the results, and scratching his head, he sat behind his desk and said, "You are clearly smart and have performed better than all the other applicants, but to be honest, you are the last person I expected to give this job to. I wanted someone more mature. However, based on the test results alone, I will give you a chance and see how you do. Do not make me regret it. Agree?"

Tania looked at him enthusiastically. "Of course. I will work hard. I promise."

Now that Tania had an office job, I began to plan my next steps. First, I became friends with her office manager.

"Please help my daughter," I told him one day. "Be critical and tough. I want her to get an education. If you challenge her, she will respond."

He did exactly that. One day, Tania called me after she left work.

"Can you believe what my boss told me today, Mom?" she said.

"What did he say?"

"That I would never be anything, but a secretary. He even criticized my clothes! Who does he think he is? I don't make the money he makes. That is not nice."

"What are you going to do?" I said.

"I'm embarrassed. I want to find another job."

"But you just started. Jumping from job to job is not good."

She took a deep breath and stayed silent for a moment.

"I know what I'm going to do," she said.

"What?"

"I will show him who he's dealing with. I will go back to school. I will prove to him that I will not be a secretary all my life."

"And what about your clothes? Do you need me to help you?"

"No. You have enough to worry about. I will go to the Salvation Army store and look for a used suit there and other office clothes. I will show him!"

I was giggling internally. The values I had instilled in her were there, and so was the drive to achieve the dream! She just needed a little push. I was not sure how far she would be willing to go to prove a point, but I was anxious to test her tenacity.

She went to the Salvation Army the very next day and bought clothes, yet going back to college required a series of steps and prerequisites. In addition, the new winter semester had just started.

"I will be ready by the fall. By then, my son will be a little older," she told me.

Phil, too, decided to go back to school. By the fall, he was enrolled in the computer-engineering program at Tampa Technical Institute. After Tania convinced college officials to allow her retroactive withdrawal from the classes she had been taking when she got pregnant, she started with a clean slate at Hillsborough Community College.

She did not know how long she would be able to work full time, raise a child, and attend college at night. Instead of signing up for an Associate's degree, she opted for a certificate program that would count towards a degree if she decided to move forward.

She could not go back to medicine, her first love, as that would take too long. Instead, after reviewing the newspapers to determine what jobs employers in Tampa were hiring for, she decided to go into accounting, a subject totally foreign to her. After the first few weeks, she called me one evening crying, "I don't understand this double-entry system, Mom. It is not logical to me. An Italian teacher by the name of Luca Pacioli invented it in 1494. It is not based on science. I hate it!"

I did not want to contradict her. "Do you know that your aunt studied accounting in addition to architecture?"

"Yes, you told me, but I don't want to bother anyone. I want to figure it out myself. I just needed to vent. That's all. Every night, I have to translate the words from English to Spanish, but because I did not study business in Cuba, the translation does not make sense either. I will just have to figure out what the instructions mean in English. I am sleeping four and five hours a night! It's frustrating."

"Pray, sweetheart. God will help you."

She took a deep breath.

“I don’t want to give up, Mom. I have so many plans for my son. I want him to go to private school one day and have the best education I can give him.”

“Big plans!” I said.

I smiled realizing that the tables had started to turn.

Chapter 17 - Married Life

Phil and I lived in a trailer park off Sheldon Road for almost five years: a single-wide with two bedrooms and two bathrooms, a tiny kitchen, and a cozy living room that hardly accommodated a sofa and a chair. It had an orange carpet and brown wood paneling on the walls that made the interior look too dark for my taste.

Sometimes, money was so tight that we lived off credit cards for months at a time. Phil and I argued about money constantly. He liked his music and enjoyed bringing home a new record occasionally, while I, accustomed to a thrifty existence, insisted on saving every penny. Life was not like I had imagined it.

Phil and I worked full time, Phil at a warehouse, and me at the hospital. My mother and my mother-in-law took turns at caring for our son and helped us as much as they could with diapers and formula for the baby.

My English was improving day by day. When I finally completed a certificate in accounting at the community college, I decided to apply somewhere else.

In searching for a suitable job, I made some mistakes. I worked for a couple of weeks at a marketing place. The owner wanted me to learn someone else's job, so he could fire that person. I could not do it. It was not in my nature. After two weeks, I told him. He gave me a one-week notice pay and I found myself jobless. I then applied at a local, family-owned air-courier company. The interview process intimidated me. The owner had one of his consultants interview me at the consultant's home.

I arrived there ready for the interview, with a portfolio and a suit. The consultant, a young man with dark hair and glasses, asked me to sit at his computer and complete a few tasks on Lotus 1,2,3, one of the first spreadsheet programs, and WordPerfect, a word-processing program. When I completed the tasks successfully, he said:

"You're good at this."

"Thank you," I answered nervously.

"Let's go to the firm where you will be working. I will introduce you to your boss."

The first thing that ran through my mind was that I was going to get stuffed into the back of a car and killed. My father had shared horrible stories about what could happen to a young woman if she was not careful. I was scared, but took a deep breath and said, "Great. What address?"

"Just follow me in your car."

This was getting interesting. I jumped into my gray, 1980 Cutlass Supreme that I'd purchased at a used-car dealership and followed him while thinking, *If only I had only brought my father with me.* After a while, we arrived at a place near Drew Park and the airport. When we parked in front of a hangar, I was still fearful for my life as I remembered the stories about human trafficking—stories that I clearly pictured as we walked into the hangar.

We climbed a set of metal stairs that led to the office. When I looked down, I noticed several men working on a small plane looking in my direction. One of them gave another man a little push and smiled at me. I immediately looked away.

Once we were inside the office, the office manager greeted me. We walked past her office to the bosses' office. He stood up immediately when he saw me.

"You must be Tania," he said with a wide smile.

So far, so good, I thought.

"I am. It is a pleasure to meet you," I said.

He went through the tasks that I would be responsible for, then introduced me to the office manager and later to the rest of the workers. He explained my role and discussed my hourly rate with me: six dollars per hour, tuition, and paid benefits for the family. When I left the office, my muscles began to relax. At last, a job with paid benefits!

I wanted to show my value to my boss and began to learn everything I could from the consultants who worked for the company. I learned how to create users in the computer system and eventually how to close the books. After a while, I became the main point of contact for the bankers. John, my boss, took notice. A few months after he hired me, he called me to his office.

"You are doing very well," he said. "I no longer need the accounting firm or IT firm I was using, so I am letting them go. I will assign those responsibilities to you and give you a three-dollar-per-hour raise. Is that okay with you?"

My eyes opened wide.

"Three dollars?" I asked.

He must have misinterpreted my reaction. "Not enough?" he asked.

"Yes, that's fine. Thank you," I said.

And just like that, my income started to increase, making my desire to learn more about how to run a company an imperative. I needed to obtain a bachelor's degree, the sooner the better. First, I decided to finish an associate of science in accounting. I studied feverishly and worked hard at the air-courier company.

A year later, I was still learning more and more in my new job. I was thirsty for expanding my knowledge. One day, unexpectedly, John invited me to lunch. Not accustomed to life in the United States, I immediately thought the worst. I called my father to let him know.

"If he tries anything funny with you, call me right away," he said.

"I will, Dad."

John and I arrived at a restaurant before the large lunch crowds, and we ordered our food. I had never been at that particular restaurant, a place that offered a fusion of Mexican and American food. I requested the cheapest thing in the menu, but I had to force myself to eat. I felt a knot on my stomach, unsure of what would happen next. After talking about our families for a while, he finally said:

"Do you know why I asked you to lunch?"

I looked at him nervously.

"Quite frankly, no."

He took a sip from his Diet Coke. "I want to offer you the office-manager position," he said.

I opened my eyes wide. "But you already have an office manager," I said.

"She won't be there much longer, not after I saw what you could do."

He bit into the last piece of chicken on his plate, swallowed it, and waited for me to say something.

"She is my friend. I cannot accept a position that will cause her to lose her job," I said.

He took a deep breath, his reddish face getting redder. "Listen very carefully, Tania. This is business. I am giving you the opportunity of a lifetime. I am paying my office manager significantly more than I pay you, for doing a fraction of what you do. You know I am a Christian man. She is my friend, but I need to make the decision that is best for the prosperity of this company. If you refuse to take this job, I will find someone who will take it."

I remained silent for a moment. This was the first and most important decision of my adult life. My family's future was at stake.

"I don't think you are giving me much of choice," I said, and remained silent for a moment. Then, I raised my head slightly and added, "I accept."

He smiled. "Great! Now, for the important part of the conversation. How much would you like to make?"

Eyebrows raised, and with a visible jolt of surprise, I said, "You want me to tell how much you should pay me?"

"Yes," he said.

Knowing well that I did not know my true value, I said, "You own the business. You tell me how much you think I'm worth." I spoke with an assertiveness I had not exhibited before.

He sighed. "Is fifteen dollars per hour okay?"

I did everything possible to hide my excitement. Fifteen dollars? A seven-dollar-an-hour raise? It was 1991. I was now a twenty-six-year old woman with a child who had just turned seven. That amount of money represented an incredible opportunity for my family, but I could not let him know how happy I was.

"That will do for now," I said, keeping my composure.

He smiled. Was he on to me?

That weekend, Phil and I visited my parents to deliver the great news.

"Fifteen dollars an hour?" my father said.

"Is your boss crazy?" asked my mother. "That is a lot of money, but do you see what happens when a smart girl like you gets an education?"

I smiled. "Yes, Mom. You told me so."

"I did."

Suddenly, Danny, our dog, and Phil Jr. ran into the house, Danny barking and Phil Jr. yelling, "I only want to play with you!"

"What are you doing to Danny?" I said.

"I was playing with his ears and patting his back, and he started barking at me and ran away," he said.

"Be gentle to him. He had an accident a few years ago, and he never recovered fully."

"I can never do anything!" yelled Phil Jr. "I'm bored!"

"He has his mother's temper," said my mother.

"Yes, Mom. Get back at me now."

She smiled and shook her head.

"Hey!" my father said. "Phil Jr. is right. I'm bored too. Let's all go to a restaurant to celebrate my daughter's big promotion."

"Yeah!" Phil Jr. cheered. "I love you, Grandpa. You are the best grandfather ever!"

"You spoil him too much, Dad," I said.

My father did his little celebratory dance.

"Fine, let's go," I said, "This time, I am paying."

"That's right!" said Phil. "You are always inviting everybody. This time, it's our turn."

"You're going to have to fight me," said my father.

Phil and I laughed.

Phil insisted on driving and took us to the Columbia Restaurant in Ybor City, an iconic, historic place located on 7th Avenue. After we sat, Phil whispered to the server that we would pick up the check.

"I'm watching you," said my father with a big smile on his face, pointing with his index and middle fingers, first to his eyes and then to Phil.

"You're not paying," said Phil. "And that's final."

We ordered paella, a traditional Spanish dish—one of my father's favorites—and the house salad. My father also ordered a pitcher of sangria for Phil and him and soft drinks for the rest of us. Being as thrifty as I was, I kept calculating in my head how much that meal was going to cost. After all, I had not started performing my new responsibilities yet. What if I didn't make it?

"Let's make a toast to my daughter on her promotion. I'm very proud of you," he said.

We toasted, my father and Phil with sangria and the rest of us with diet drinks. When the steamy paella finally arrived, it was worth the wait. The mixture of chicken, pork, seafood, yellow rice, and spices smelled and tasted delicious. It was a dish that married Cuban and Spanish flavors into a heavenly mix well suited for a king. We ate, drank, and celebrated the joy of living in the United States. After the first pitcher of sangria was finished, my father ordered a second one.

"That's too much, Rio. Just order water," protested my mother.

"I'm not driving. Stop complaining. This is a celebration."

My father practically drank the second pitcher by himself, while my mother watched him. When he poured the last glass, she crossed her arms and stared at him. He lifted his glass, smiled, glanced at my mother, and said:

"To my family!"

She rolled her eyes and shook her head.

***

Becoming office manager pushed my career to a new level. I had already finished my associate's degree and had transferred to the University of South Florida to obtain a bachelor's degree in accounting.

Phil was moving forward, too. He graduated from Tampa Technical Institute with a bachelor's in computer engineering and was working for a subsidiary of IBM. Two years before, we had sold the trailer and moved into our first house. Nothing fancy. Three small bedrooms, one bathroom, and a tiny kitchen. The house had been burned down and rebuilt, and we bought it for a good price.

The day of the closing, when we opened the door to our new home, Phil Jr. ran in, explored each corner of the house, and yelled from one of the rooms, "This is my room! This is my room!" We followed him. He was standing in the middle of a newly carpeted area, wide-eyed, a smile on his face. His creamy white cheeks had turned slightly pink from all the running.

"And look, Mom and Dad! I can see the backyard from my room! It's big! Can we get a dog?"

Phil and I smiled and embraced. At last, a real home for our new family!

We tried to get little Phil a dog. We looked through the classified section and found a couple that was giving one away, but when we brought it home, we realized the dog was bigger than Phil Jr. The moment we let the big, black dog lose in the backyard, little Phil yelled: "Come on, doggie. Let's play!"

The dog charged towards little Phil at full speed and knocked him down on the grass. Our son was crying and screaming. Phil and I looked at each other.

"We have to take it back," I said.

The new pet only lasted a day at our house, and Phil Jr. did not ask for a dog ever again.

Having a new position with a significantly higher paycheck did not deter me from my thrifty ways. If anything, it motivated to watch every penny with even more tenacity. Remembering my mother's advice, I began to send additional principal payments to the lender. I became obsessed with paying our mortgage off.

Chapter 18 - Dad

My parent's home in Town and Country, a modest frame house with three bedrooms and one bathroom, had a big yard and was always full of people. The rooms were tiny, so my father knocked out a wall and combined two bedrooms to have a larger master bedroom where his grandchildren could play.

The family kept growing. Gustavo found his future wife shortly after high school, and by the year 1996, my parents already had three grandchildren, two from Lynette's marriage, and Phil Jr. Lynette's husband, Tony, worked for my father, and they had a wonderful relationship. Phil had gained some acceptance from Dad after their rough beginnings, although they argued frequently. Dad had left-leaning tendencies and Phil was more aligned with the Republican ideals.

Phil and I continued to make progress at work, which had allowed us to move to a house in the Carrollwood area, after selling our first home for a decent profit. I did not use a real estate agent, but handled the entire transaction myself. With the savings, I bought myself an upright piano, something I'd wanted since my arrival to the United States.

Phil and I decided to sell a Ford Taurus we had purchased a few years earlier to my father. It had low miles and was in excellent condition. My father had loved that car since the moment he saw it, and when Phil told him he would sell it to him, my father looked like he had won the lottery. It was worth more than double the price Dad paid for it.

From the day we transferred ownership of the car to my father, it became his most valued possession. He was always cleaning it. It was his baby.

My father was finally happy, but his habits continued, especially the drinking and the smoking, while my mother, realizing she could not change him, looked the other way.

He was a good grandfather, always playing with his three grandchildren–all boys–and buying gifts for them. Dad bought them ice cream, made them his famous pizzas, played catch with them, anything to please them. The kids reciprocated by giving him their love and smiling from ear to ear when their grandfather played with them in the yard, or when he made faces at them.

Dad still did his little dance of jubilation when he was happy and, as always, remained the joy of every gathering—until one day.

He had just turned fifty-nine a couple of months before, and we had celebrated his birthday at a restaurant in Clearwater Beach with the entire family except for my Aunt Berta and her family, who still lived in Miami. My uncle worked as an engineer and my aunt as an accountant. They were too busy with their lives and only came to Tampa every Christmas.

The mysterious calls had stopped years before. Everything seemed perfect, except for the look on my father's eyes during his birthday lunch. I could feel he was hiding something behind his smile. One night, our telephone rang in the middle of the night.

"Hurry home!" my mother screamed hysterically. "Your father had a stroke and was taken by ambulance to the hospital. Please hurry and pick me up."

We rushed out of our house with Phil Jr. still half asleep. First, we picked up my mother, who was still crying inconsolably when we arrived, and then we headed towards my in-laws' home to drop off our twelve-year-old. On the way there, as he noticed his grandmother's anguish, he asked a couple of times, "Is Grandpa going to be okay, Grandma?"

She burst into tears each time.

"Phil Jr., stop bothering your grandmother. Go back to sleep. We will wake you up when you get to your grandparents' house."

He did not listen. Through the mirror on the passenger side, I could see him talking to his grandmother, until she embraced him and said, with her voice cracking, "I know how much you love your grandfather, Phil Jr. He will be okay."

I called my sister and my brother before leaving my in-laws' house, and by the time we arrived at Tampa General Hospital, they were there with their spouses. We all embraced each other.

"What happened to Dad, Mom? Was he sick?" asked my brother. He was a mirror image of my father when he was the same age.

"He visited the doctor recently, after I insisted I don't know how many times, and was diagnosed with emphysema. He smoked too much and would not stop. The doctors said he had the lungs of an eighty-year-old."

"Why didn't you tell us?" he asked.

"You know your father. He never wanted you to worry. He wanted to portray the strong man he always was."

"Stop talking as if he were dead!" yelled my sister. "He's not dead."

"I'm sorry," Mom said. "You are right. We need to remain positive and pray for him."

We anxiously waited for the doctor to come out. Eventually, my mother was allowed to go into our father's room, but when fifteen minutes had passed and we did not hear anything from her, I could not wait any longer and managed to sneak into his room. I was not ready for what I found.

When I entered, my father's mouth was twisted. He looked pale and unrecognizable, with a breathing tube, an IV, and a blood-pressure cuff connected to him.

"Oh my God!" I said. "Why does he look like that, Mom! Is he going to be okay?"

She stood up and embraced me. I let her, and we cried in each other's arms.

"Let it out sweetheart," she said. "I know how much your father means to you. It's good to let it out."

I did, like never before.

By the time my father left the hospital, he was not himself. He could not walk or speak, but his mind was intact. I picked him up at the hospital, and one of the workers helped lift him into the passenger side of my new Honda Civic. The worker folded the wheelchair and placed it in the back seat, as my trunk was too small. Mom squeezed into the back seat as well.

On the way home, we stopped at a light, and my father noticed a wrinkled woman who was driving a car next to us. She was much older than he. He began to make noises to get my attention. Once I looked in his direction, he pointed at the woman repeatedly, and then at his useless legs. Then, he brought his index finger to his temple, as if he were carrying a gun, and mimicked the movement of firing.

"You're going to be fine, Dad. This is temporary. You can't think that way," I told him.

He shook his head, tears running down his face. Then, he slammed the passenger door with his fist.

My father remained in a wheelchair for almost a year and still could not speak. He had never been a religious man, but one day, to the surprise of the nurses at the rehabilitation center where I took him, he noticed he could sing "Ave Maria." All the nurses cried when they heard him sing. Since then, when we had family gatherings, we would tell him:

"Come on, Dad. Sing 'Ave Maria.'" He did each time.

"Great job!" we would say, applauding. "You'll see, Dad. Soon, you will be able to talk again."

But my father never spoke or walked again. A major stroke ended his life shortly after he turned sixty.

My mother went into a deep state of depression after his death, similar to the state she had been in when I was a child and she'd tried to end her life. He had been only man she'd ever loved.

One day, she told me, "I can't live without your father. I just can't. All of you are grown up and married. You don't need me anymore."

All the memories from my childhood flooded my mind. Not again, not again. I stared at my mother silently, my expression contorted with anger.

"Mom," I said. "I have kept this to myself for years." I took a deep breath. "It has been eating me inside, but no more. Do you remember the day you tried to kill yourself? I was six years old, anxious to see you and tell you about my day. But instead, I had to rush out of the house to ask the neighbors for help. For years, I lived with the nightmares, the night terrors. That experience changed my life in ways you never imagined. I never wanted to love anyone again. I had loved my father, and he left Cuba. I loved you, and you wanted to leave me. I loved Aunt Berta and her family, my friends in Cuba, and had to leave them too. I loved my grandmother, and she too left me. I told myself that I would not ever love anyone again because in the end, everyone leaves. That is how I coped, by not getting close, not even to my husband or my son. I can't live like this anymore. If you insist on this nonsense, I will not stop you this time. I can't continue to live with the fear that you too will check out of my life before it's time. Not anymore!"

After these words, she looked at me for a while, as if not knowing what to say. "I never knew you still remembered. Is that why you were so distant?"

I looked down.

"So, you were distant because you loved me," she said. "You did not want to get hurt again."

She took a deep breath and shook her head. "I have been so wrong all these years," she said. "I am so sorry I did this to you. I wanted to believe you had forgotten. My poor child. What a burden to live with."

She walked towards me and embraced me. I let her.

"I want to make you a promise," she said. "This is the last time I will say anything about leaving this world. I now understand how much you need me. I am so sorry."

My mother was true to her word, and to my surprise, she kept my father's business. My sister's husband still worked for her and fulfilled my father's duties with all the knowledge he had acquired from my father, and she procured customers and even learned how to measure. She still could not drive. My father had scared her so much when he tried to teach her that she never learned.

On a few occasions, after I finished at work, or on weekends, I accompanied her to customers' houses. My brother and my sister helped as much as they could. The customers acted surprised to see an old, sick woman with an accent taking measurements. But my mother was strong, stubborn, and resourceful and refused to live off anybody, not even her children.

My mother's health deteriorated rapidly after my father passed away. Breathing became difficult, and cough attacks the norm. Not even the cannula connected to her nostrils to supply her with oxygen stopped her from turning purple during each attack. Her doctors ordered a number of tests to try to identify the cause. Even in such a condition, she still continued to work and visit customers.

Four years after my father passed away, my mother was diagnosed with carcinoid tumors of the lungs, a form of cancer. We obtained the opinions of several doctors about how long she had to live. "Six months," they agreed. There was no known treatment for her condition. My siblings and I were crushed.

My mother called me the Saturday morning after her diagnosis. "We must start to document my story," she told me. "There is no time to lose. People need to know what happened to our family."

"That is the last thing you need to worry about!" I protested. "I want you to get better."

"I know how much you and your siblings love me, but your love cannot save me. Not this time. Let's focus on documenting my story. You have to promise me that you will publish it one day. The world has to know what happened to us when we lived in Cuba."

"Fine, fine! I promise," I said.

I started to meet with my mother as much as my time allowed, and she, too, began to write about her life in journals and letters.

By then, I was working as a finance manager at Tampa General Hospital, and after hearing about all the miracles the workers at that hospital performed every day, I could not accept that she was going to die. I needed to do something. She needed a miracle.

During my frequent nights of insomnia, I would sit on my sofa while Phil and Phil Jr. slept, open my laptop, and feverishly research her condition: carcinoid tumors of the lungs. I read every article and saved hundreds of pages of research.

Just when I had started to become discouraged, I read about Sandostatin, a fairly new drug that was helping patients with carcinoids of the intestines. None of the trials involved carcinoids of the lungs.

I brought my documentation to Dr. Fields, her new cancer doctor. He had a practice in Armenia Avenue and was young, of Chinese origin, and very kind. Even if my mother had no cure and was going to die, she preferred dealing with a doctor who showed compassion towards his patients. Neither my mother nor I had liked the defeatist approach of her previous cancer doctor.

"Could you try these shots?" I asked Dr. Fields.

He smiled at me with compassion and embraced me. He was the most caring doctor I had ever met, always hugging his patients, and even the patients' relatives. Later, I understood why. His mother, too, had died of cancer.

"Tania, this is not a proven treatment for her specific condition. I am so sorry."

"Dr. Fields, if she were your mother, wouldn't you do everything you could to save her? Wouldn't you at least try? Please read these materials. Look, at least read this paragraph!"

I showed him a highlighted section. He read it quickly. He took a deep breath and nodded.

"You are right. I would have done anything to keep my mother alive. I will prescribe the shots and have my staff work with her insurance. It will be an uphill battle with the insurance, as this is not an accepted treatment for her condition."

That was a defining moment in my mother's life. These shots helped extend her life for years, much longer than initially anticipated. That was the second time I'd saved her (and of course, Dr. Fields, a doctor who was willing to listen). Years later, we learned that my mother's case would be studied by other physicians and that Sandostatin would become the treatment of choice to treat carcinoids of the lungs.

My father's death and my mother's illness transformed my family. It was as if part of the glue that held it together had dissipated. My brother divorced his first wife when they could not conceive a family. My sister also divorced her husband.

After a couple of years, when Gustavo and his ex-wife realized they could not live without each other, they remarried, and thanks to the advanced science of artificial insemination, they were blessed with twins.

My mother was the happiest grandmother on earth when the twins were born. Some years later, she would meet another granddaughter. My brother had impregnated a woman when he was seventeen and learned about his daughter after the twins were born. The girl was almost a teenager by the time she met her father.

The monthly Sandostatin shots allowed my mother to see her six grandchildren grow and her children succeed in America.

After a while, my sister met a man of Irish background who had three children from his first marriage, and she married him. Strangely enough, he lived right next to my brother's house, in a beautiful gated community. By then, she had been working at the billing and medical-records office of a large Tampa hospital for years.

With the knowledge my brother had gained when he helped my father in his shop, he obtained a job as a manager of a glass company. He continued to train and perfect his knowledge of glass techniques and developed a special program to price jobs. After a few years, he was featured in trade magazines for his expertise.

As for me, I still loved learning. Once I started the university, I could not get enough, and I finished two masters' degrees, which allowed me to become the accounting director at the hospital where I had worked as a manager. No matter how much I made, I always maintained my thrifty ways.

By the time the real estate bubble began to burst, starting around 2007, Phil and I had finished paying off our house. In 2010, the market was flooded with inexpensive short sales, and we began to invest in residential real estate.

Mom had stayed in the Town and Country house for several years. She did not want to leave because that home reminded her of my father. As her condition worsened, I convinced her to move to a block house. I wanted her to have a nice place before she died. I wrote this on the last day she lived in the Town and Country house. By then, I was taking creative-writing classes at the University of South Florida. I needed to perfect the craft of writing a novel in order to fulfill her wishes. This essay, entitled "The Shop," earned me an A.

Today, I am opening papá's shop, the place I avoided for seven years after his premature death, the place that was born out of a $10,000 workers' compensation settlement a few years ago after a pallet of glass fell on his back and nearly killed him.

When I open the double wooden doors, they make a creaking noise that sends chills all the way to my bones. I enter slowly. Everything is still the way I remembered, except for the layers of thick dust and elaborate designs of spider webs that cover the windows, the ceilings, and machines. In front of me is a large rectangular table covered with carpet material where he placed the glass to make it easier to maneuver. It was there where he created glass swans, clocks, and containers he sold to catering firms, individuals, hotels, even strip bars. Papá didn't discriminate.

I still remember his smile the first day he received a $1,000 check from a hotel near downtown. He took all of *us all to a seafood restaurant in Clearwater Beach to celebrate. I was so proud of him. He sat across from me drinking a Michelob Light, smoking More Menthols. The smoke created a shield between us, but his happiness filtered right through it and enveloped me like a tornado, making me feel strangely safe.*

I look down and, on the concrete floor, notice several cigarette butts. Then I focus my attention on the table where an empty beer bottle has been waiting for seven years for his return. I take a broom and begin to wipe the spider webs from the walls and ceilings, and I think about my purpose here today. When I do, I feel this knot in my stomach because my job, the reason why I'm entering this place, is to clean it, to remove every machine, every piece of glass, every cutting instrument, even the table where he worked. My purpose today is to wipe from existence the place that fed him and mamá for several years after I left home. A contractor is buying the shop and the house to convert them into apartments and rent them to someone who would never know the shop's history. We are moving mamá, who is sick and older now, closer to her children because, in a way, her children have become the adults and she the child.

Mamá didn't want to sell the house at first; she wanted to hold on to the memories of my father, to the place they shared for so many years, but I convinced her it was the best thing to do. I convinced her that a dirty shop rotting away won't bring papá back.

I never realized, now that I have cleared the shop, how difficult it would be to close its doors for the last time.

Chapter 19 - Mom

Since our arrival to the United States, Mom had always lived in frame houses, since that was all she could afford. These older houses made her severe allergies more difficult to control.

I found one made of concrete block with two bedrooms, two bathrooms, an inside laundry, a nice kitchen with a small bar that accommodated three bar stools, and a screened lanai leading to a fenced yard where her grandchildren could play.

I quickly contacted the real estate agent and scheduled an appointment. I could not wait to show it to my mother.

When we walked into the cozy Carrollwood home, Mother raised her eyebrows and opened her eyes wide.

"Are you sure I can afford it?" she asked. "It is beautiful!"

"It is $15,000 outside of your price range, but I will give you the difference."

She shook her head. "Oh no! I will not accept anything from you or any of my children," she said firmly, but her last word was drowned in repeated coughs. I patted her on her back until her coughing ceased.

"Mom, please. I want you to be happy. I know how much you like this home."

"It's true that I never imagined myself in a place like this," she said. "But that does not mean I will take advantage of my children."

"Mom, I want to do this, so there is nothing else to discuss. I will give you the rest of the money."

"Correction," she said. "You will lend me the money. I will pay you every dollar back. You have to give me the satisfaction that I accomplished this myself."

I took a deep breath.

"Fine, Mom. I will lend it to you."

"With formal papers!" she added. "If something happens to me, I don't want any fighting between you, your brother, and your sister."

"That will never happen, Mom. You raised us well."

My words seemed to take her by surprise.

"Well, I definitely did everything I could, but some of you, and I won't say who, are more hardheaded than others."

"Are you still angry that I married Phil?" I asked.

She took a deep breath. "No, but I am still angry that I never saw you in a wedding dress," she said, crossing her arms.

"How many people have you seen spending money on a wedding and a beautiful dress, only to have a marriage that does not last?" I asked. "So, is it really that important?"

"For me, it is!" she said firmly, and nodded. "You will never convince me otherwise."

"And you tell me that I'm a hardhead?"

We laughed. It was set. I gave her the additional money for the house, but I knew she could not afford to pay me back. Doing so would mean taking away from her food, and I would never allow that.

I asked her for her bank-account information and began to make small transfers into her account until she discovered the extra money.

“Why do I have more money in my account than what I deposit?” she asked one day during my weekly visit.

“Why are you asking me?” I said.

“Please stop doing it. Don’t make me upset,” my mother said.

“Why does it have to be me? It is probably my brother.”

She took shook her head. “You make me angry,” she said.

When my father was alive, Mom seldom went anywhere because they never had sufficient disposable income. Years earlier, after Phil and I started to travel around the world, she could not wait to hear about my trips. She would even make me write a daily journal and share it with her via e-mail. I wrote her from China, Italy, France, and Germany.

“I am cruising on the Danube River on a Viking Cruise ship,” I would write.

“Tell me more. What do you see?” she would reply, happy as a child with a lollipop.

I knew how much she wanted to experience the world, so I began to book some trips for her, one of them to see the popular Cuban singer Willy Chirino aboard a cruise ship heading for the Bahamas. I had never seen her so happy before, especially when he sang “Ya Viene Llegando,” a song that gave hope that Cuba would soon be free. The way she smiled and lifted her arms in the air while she sang along with the rest of the crowd, the manner in which she moved her body to the rhythm, allowing herself to be carried away, the miraculous way in which her cough disappeared during the time she was at the concert, suggested to me that in her mind, these songs had transported her to our home on Zapote Street, but not to the place we left. Our home in Havana was now freshly painted and did not have peeling walls and moldy ceilings supported by wood trusses. She was on the porch serving her four grandchildren *café con leche* and did not need a ration card to buy food. Mom could travel out of the country when she wished, without government restrictions, and she could speak her mind, without having to hide in a room without windows. *That* was the Cuba she was transported to as she sang.

My mother had always dreamed of visiting Paris. I contacted a travel agency and they paired her with other single women. She packed all her medications and met with her doctor in advance. I was afraid at first, thinking that it would be difficult to travel in her condition, but even the preparation for this trip gave her life and hope. Mom toured Europe and stayed in Paris for a couple of nights.

When she returned from her trip, she developed her pictures to show me all she had seen. There was one in particular taken at night in front of the lit-up Eiffel Tower. She was wearing a heavy jacket and smiled as she pointed at the tower, while the wind played with her hair. The happiness pouring from her made her appear ten years younger.

Phil and I also took her and my in-laws to Spain, as my mother wanted to see the place where her father was born. That trip almost cost me my life.

We had to flown to Madrid, where we stayed a couple of nights, and from there a tour bus drove us to various cities in the southern portion of Spain. Each day, we spent the night in a different town: Seville, Cordoba, Costa del Sol, even the English territory of Gibraltar.

When we arrived in Seville, the sun was scorching hot: 107 degrees. I was dragging my large piece of luggage towards the entrance of the hotel, along with other passengers. Ahead of me was a revolving door, and in front of it, a carpeted area. My foot got stuck in the carpet, while I stumbled down to the floor. My upper body fell as the door turned. Everything happened fast. The passengers were paralyzed when they saw me. A few women screamed.

Phil saw me on the ground, the revolving door coming towards me. Suddenly, he threw himself in front of it to attempt to stop it. He pushed it as hard as he could, but the safety mechanism designed to stop it did not work. Moments later, he realized he was losing the battle and thought it was over. Still, he kept pushing his body against the door to protect me. He closed his eyes, embraced me, and waited for the worst. Suddenly the door stopped, just before it crushed us both.

My mother and the other passengers had witnessed the entire incident in horror. For the rest of the vacation, I was a celebrity with my tour group for all the wrong reasons.

Later that afternoon, as I sat on a sofa in the lobby, my swollen knee black and blue, Phil and my mother on either side of me, Phil Jr. playing with Legos by a glass coffee table, my mother looked at Phil and said, “Thank you for risking your life for Tania. You are a good man, and she is lucky to have you.”

My mother never questioned my decision to marry Phil again.

Chapter 20 - My New Home

It is the year 2011. My husband, Rio, passed away several years ago, in 1997. I am sitting on the sofa watching a young couple working outside. She is mute; he shows signs of mental retardation, but they both play with each other while they pick up the leaves on my lawn. I can no longer do it, as my condition has worsened, even more now that I decided to stop getting the shots of Sandostatin.

I cannot help but to envy the happiness of the couple working in my yard. It takes so little to be happy, and yet we insist in finding reasons not to be.

"Why are you doing this, Mom?" Tania yelled at me after we left my doctor's office. "You know you are going to die if you stop the shots."

I smiled at her. "I'm done, sweetheart. The medication has side effects. I am a diabetic, and look at me. My heart is no longer working right. I am swollen all the time. I am seventy-two years old. I have had a long, beautiful life. I have amazing, successful children and wonderful grandchildren. I am thankful to God for these things."

"We need you, Mom," she said, with her eyes full of tears. My Tania, my sweet, hardheaded, and kind Tania. I misunderstood her for so many years.

"You don't need me anymore, my love," I said.

She looked the other way and did not say anything at first. I could hear her irregular breathing and noticed her wiping her eyes before she turned to me.

"Are you hungry?" she asked me. "What would you like to eat? I will buy whatever you want."

She brought her index finger to her face and wiped another tear.

"Buy me a big, breaded steak. That is what I want."

She forced a smile. "Of course, anything, Mom," she said, her voice breaking.

That weekend, Tania took me to the second rental home she and Phil had purchased. They had created a small business, while they still worked their regular jobs, Tania as a director of accounting, and Phil, as a contract administrator. I was hooked up to my oxygen tank when I entered the house. The handyman was painting it when we walked in, a light cream color throughout.

"The house looks beautiful, like your first rental. I cannot believe that my daughter is a businesswoman like me."

"You taught me well, Mom."

"I sure did," I said proudly. "I just wish your brother and sister had a business too."

"They will, Mom," she said. "One day, they will. Don't worry."

"I am proud of you, Tania. Now, I can die in peace."

"Why would you say that? Stop talking that way!"

I changed the subject, but the way I was feeling, I realized I needed to hurry. There was so much I had not shared with Tania, so much that I wanted to tell my children and grandchildren. I went home, took out one of my journals, and began to write. My time was running out.

Now, as I sit by my window looking at this couple, realizing my days on this earth are few, memories flash before my eyes. Rio and I fought about so many small things during the few years we were together, when we had so much to be thankful for.

Life passes so quickly. One day, Rio and I were riding on Rio's motorcycle on El Malecón, Havana's waterfront, at full speed. We were young and happy, afraid of nothing. The warm Caribbean ocean breeze caressed our bodies, while the waters splashed the rocks by the sea wall. Sometime later, our three little treasures came to this world, one after the other. I wanted them to grow up in a free country. And who doesn't want the best for their children? That decision took twelve years from my life, but in retrospect, I had something Rio did not. I was blessed to see them say their first words, to take their first steps, to write their first letters and numbers.

Life is temporary glimpses of happiness. It is about loving with intensity and leaving a mark in the world. Its fleeting nature is not to be feared, but to be embraced with every fiber of our being, with the knowledge that tomorrow does not belong to us, yet it may be shaped by us with simple gestures of kindness.

I learned that a little too late.

Chapter 21 - The Dance

My mother never asked for much, but one day, she told me: “Don’t ever take me to a nursing home. I want to die here, within these walls.”

The uncharacteristic calm tone of her voice and the resignation in her gaze echoed a premonition. I shared my concerns with Lynette and Gustavo, and we agreed to spend as much time as we could with her, especially my brother, who worked closer to her house.

One day, when I stopped by her house after work to deliver a bag of groceries, she asked me to sit down for a moment. She had something important to tell me.

“Is there something wrong with your brother?” she asked me as we sat next to each other on her green leather sofa.

“Why do you ask?”

“Every day he comes here, brings me lunch, and talks to me for an hour.”

“What’s wrong with that?” I asked. “He’s a good son.”

She waved her hand back in dismissal.

“Gustavo has never done that before. He’s hiding something. I think he and his wife are having problems. After all, they are on their second marriage to each other. If it did not work the first time, what makes them think it is going to work the second time?”

I smiled. “No, Mom. They love each other very much. They realized that when they divorced the first time. Now they have two kids and they are very happy.”

She shook her head.

“I still think he is hiding something.”

“The older you get, the funnier you get,” I said.

She crossed her arms. “I am not kidding. Something is wrong. You still think you know it all, but I am older and smarter than you.”

I laughed. “No argument here, Mom.”

“You don’t understand,” she said. “I am his mother. If he is having a problem, I should know.”

I kissed her on the cheek and reassured her he was fine, but it did not help.

That night, while I cooked dinner for Phil and Phil Jr., my mother and I spoke again, like we did every night. She had talked to my brother, but disregarding what he told her, she kept theorizing about the problems in his marital life. When I finally managed to change the subject, her next topic concerned me.

“I had a dream about my mother last night,” she said. “She told me that everything was going to be alright. I am not sure if she was referring to Gustavo.” She paused for a moment. “My father was standing next to her, but I did not see Rio. I miss him, Tania. You should have seen your father when I first met him: his brown boots on his desk, his thin body and dreamy eyes all the ladies loved. He was out of my league, you know, but I could not help it. I fell in love with him the moment I saw him. He was dating someone else and was going to marry her, but when she told him she could not give him a family, he left her. That was when he noticed me.”

Mom also talked about her sister, Berta. “What a temper!” she would tell me. “I don’t know how her husband can take it!”

I knew she did not mean that. Mom always knew everything about everyone, but no matter what she said, her actions revealed what was in her heart —like her many donations to St. Jude's Children Hospital and the Shriner's Hospital and the party she threw at our house in Cuba for a girl who had a schizophrenic mother and a mute, mentally-disturbed brother. The girl, her sister, her brother, and her parents lived in a tiny one-bedroom apartment. Mom took some of the little money she had saved from dealing in the black market and gave her a night to remember. That was my mother. She was like an angel sent by God himself, a rose in an empty garden.

Phil and I stayed up late watching a show on HBO one night. A couple of hours later, about one, my telephone rang. I rushed to pick it up.

"Hello?"

"Tania," a male voice said.

"Yes?"

"It's Gustavo," he said, his voice cracking. "I'm calling about Mom."

"What happened?"

"The paramedics are here to take her to the hospital. She's not breathing. Please don't drive yourself. Have Phil drive you."

"Oh, my God! Oh my God! Not Mom. Tell me, please. Tell me it's not true."

He remained silent for a moment. "Just hurry. Lynette is on the way."

And after those words, he hung up.

I rushed to our bedroom. "Phil, I have to go to the hospital. My mom is being taken there by ambulance. You stay here with Phil Jr."

Phil did not hear me. I kept shaking him until he opened his eyes.

"What's wrong?" he said and yawned.

"She's not breathing."

"What are you talking about? Who?"

"Mom!"

"Oh, no!" Phil said as he quickly got up and caressed my arm. "I am so sorry. Let me go with you."

"Come later. Sleep a few more hours."

I did not wait for him to answer and went to the bathroom to wash my face. I needed to hurry.

For days, my mother was between life and death, and the doctors placed her in an induced coma. They wanted to take her off the ventilator after a while, but they did not know what was going to happen when and if she woke up.

"We will need to place her in a home," Gustavo told me one night.

"No one is taking Mother out of the house," I said sternly. "You hear?"

"But none of us can take care of her. We all work," he said.

"Even if I have to take all the money I have to have someone care for her at her house, I will do that. I promised her!" I said, and burst into tears.

He stayed silent, and Lynette, not used to seeing me cry, came to my side and embraced me. As she patted me on the back, she told my brother: "Stop upsetting my little sister," that was what she always called me as we were growing up, "Mom is not going anywhere. It's two of us against one."

My sister was always on my side, but my brother had the biggest heart of all of us. He had inherited the rough exterior of my father, and was soft as vanilla custard inside. We did not argue again about where my mother was going to go, if and when she left the hospital.

At last, the day she was going to be disconnected from her breathing machine arrived. Gustavo, Lynette, and I later argued whether this was the right decision, but in the end, we trusted the doctors' recommendations.

We called her cousin, whom she loved like a brother, so he could talk to her if she woke up. My aunt Berta was driving from Miami, but we could not wait for her to arrive. As the doctors began to disconnect her from the tubes, we held hands and prayed. Her grandchildren were all outside in the waiting room. My in-laws also waited outside.

Suddenly, after the machine was disconnected, she took a deep breath.

"Mom?" asked my brother. "Are you okay?"

"I am," she said. "What happened?"

The doctor and the nurse in the room seemed dumbfounded, and so were we.

"Mom, you died and came back," said my sister.

"Why are you holding the telephone?" asked my mother.

"Your cousin is on the phone."

"Rogelio?"

"Yes."

"Let me talk to him."

She picked up the handset.

The doctor talked to my brother briefly and stepped out of the room, while the nurse took my mother's blood pressure and left.

"Someone will be monitoring her," she said, before she exited the room. "But if you need anything, please press the button."

"Rogelio, from what I hear, I have a second chance at life," my mother said after the nurse left. She was happy, as if she had awoken from a bad dream to find out it was not real. "So before I lose this chance, I need to tell everyone what is on my mind. Don't argue with me this time. You know that you have always been like my brother, but when I leave this earth for good, please go to Miami and be with your family. Family is the most important thing there is."

She paused for a moment.

"Come on, *chico*. No reason to cry. This is a happy moment. I'm back."

They spoke for a while longer, and when she finished, she ordered:

"Now, I want to talk to each of my grandchildren, in private," she said.

"For what?" my brother asked.

"None of your business. You have your ways to deal with your children, and I have mine. I want to talk to each one of you as well."

"Whatever you want, Mom," I said, looking at my brother and signaling with one hand not to argue.

"Yes, Captain Laura," said my sister, jokingly. "As you wish."

My mother spent the rest of that day and part of the next speaking to each of her children and grandchildren to tell them what to do upon her death. Each had strict orders from my mother that no one should disclose their private conversation with anyone else. When it was my turn, my mother made promise again that if something happened to her, she wanted to die at home, no matter what my brother said. Once again, I told her not to worry. She also made me promise that I would publish a book about her life.

"We've met many times, but there are things I have not told you. Everything is written," she said.

"Don't worry. I will publish your story."

"It is important you do. And about my house, don't sell it. Rent it, and if the grandkids need money, do what you feel is right to help them with the income it generates. Remember my rule: never give your children the fish, but teach them how to fish."

"I have not forgotten."

"And take care of your brother and sister. Never fight with each other, and be there for each other, always."

"We will, Mom." I said.

"If they had only created their own businesses," she said.

"You never know, Mom. There is still time."

"There is one more thing," she said. "I have already paid for my casket and left money for my funeral. I did not want to be a burden. Also, after I die—and I know this will sound a little weird—I will make my presence known to you. Be aware of your surroundings. You will be able to feel me, but neither your brother nor sister will."

"I know you believe in spirits, Mom, but I don't. That sounds really creepy."

"When I come to you, you will know," she said, and sighed. "We have a very special connection. Twice you saved my life! You are my little angel. And just know this: wherever you are, I will always be there with you," she said, taking my hands between hers and smiling.

"Do we have to keep talking about death?" I asked, fearful that my emotions would betray me.

"We all have to die one day," she said. "Don't be so afraid to talk about it. It is as normal as breathing. It is good to tell each other what is in our hearts before we leave this world forever. This way, there are no regrets."

I remained silent and looked down.

"Come here, my guardian angel," she said. "Hug me."

I raised my head slowly and our eyes met. With a loud sob, I threw myself into the arms of my mother. Our embrace lasted for a long while, revealing, uncovering feelings buried inside me for way too long.

***

It was another busy month-end close, as I examined the results for the billion-dollar hospital. My assistant walked in to ask me about an upcoming meeting. "What time would you prefer?" she asked. "After lunch or early morning is best," I said.

She left, and I continued to work, carefully reviewing each number against actual and budget, walking in and out of my office to ask about specific invoices, calling the department heads to request explanations regarding increases to the budget.

As I picked up a document from my printer, I casually glanced at the two pictures on my credenza, one of Phil, Phil Jr., and me, the second of Mom, Dad, and the entire family.

I could not believe that Phil and I had been married for twenty-eight years. So much had changed since 1983. For the first time in history, the United States had elected a black president. With all the propaganda I'd heard when I was growing up in Cuba, I never thought that would happen. I was not fond of Obama's policies. However, as an American citizen, I believed that the voters had spoken, and I respected and admired the democratic system of my adopted country.

Our son no longer lived with us. After completing graduate studies at the University of South Florida, he had moved to the Upper East Side in New York City and worked in the financial district. My Aunt Berta had moved from Miami to Orlando. Her two daughters had children by then, and the family kept growing and prospering. Both of my aunt's daughters had completed graduate studies–the younger had an engineering degree from Duke. The elder was a CPA.

Our entire family had embraced the promise of America with every fiber of our beings. Life was good. I had traveled the world with Phil. It took us a few years to be able to afford these trips, but when we started to travel frequently, I could not get enough. I felt free when we visited other countries, experienced new cultures, and met new people. My mother loved to hear about our trips.

When we were not traveling, life was routine: family and work primarily.

On this particular day, I was not worried about anything other than my month-end close. But that was about to change.

After the telephone rang, I looked at the caller identification–it seemed familiar, but I was not sure. I picked up the handset, afraid it was one of the many vendors who called about offering their services. I did not have time to talk to vendors–too much on my plate.

"Is this Tania Mendez?" A female voice said.

"Yes, this is she." I said.

"We are calling from St. Joseph's Hospital," the voice said. "It's about your mother."

I closed my eyes, suspecting what would come next.

"She called 911. By the time the ambulance came, she had to be revived, but she is here now. We are doing everything we can. You should come right away and notify your loved ones. Her condition is critical."

"Oh my God!" I cried. I dropped the handset and began to sob uncontrollably. "Not my Mom, God! Not my Mom," I said, choking in my tears.

My office was located in the executive suite area, and one of the vice presidents who had just arrived rushed into my office when he heard me.

"Is everything okay?"

I shook my head, my eyelashes clumped together, my face reddened and wet with my tears.

"It's my Mom! She's dying! I need to be with her. I have to go!" I began to gather my belongings frantically.

"You are in no condition to drive," he said. "Leave your car here. I will drive you myself."

"But you're busy. I don't want to impose."

"We are all family here, Tania, and family is more important than anything," he said.

I never forgot his kindness, and as he drove me to the hospital, I called everyone in the family: my sister, my brother, my husband, my in-laws, Aunt Berta, Mom's cousin, my son. Each time I delivered the news, I would break into tears.

My coworker made believe he was not hearing what I was saying to give me some privacy, but his expression remained somber and concerned as he drove. When we arrived at the hospital, he assured me: "If there is anything I can do, please do not hesitate to call me. We are all here for you. I will call your boss when I get back. Don't worry about anything, only your mom."

His words had the effect of warm *café con leche* in the morning. I could tell he meant what he said, and it was comforting to know that I worked at a place that valued my family and me.

My siblings and I arrived at practically the same time, and we embraced each other.

During the next thirty hours, we never left her alone. Late at night, my brother insisted that my sister and I go home to shower and sleep a few hours. He would stay at the hospital. My blood pressure had started to spike and I felt physically and mentally exhausted. My sister and I left my brother at the hospital, as he suggested, and we drove home, but I could not sleep much.

At two, I drove back to the hospital. By then, Phil and I lived in Odessa, a suburb of Tampa located about twenty miles from the hospital where Mom was taken. I took the Veterans Expressway to get there faster, and as I contemplated the mostly deserted highway, I told myself:

"Today is the day of my mother's death." I just knew.

When I arrived, I tried to get my brother to go home, but he refused.

The doctor came in the morning and said that my mother did not have brain function any longer. He asked us to make a decision about what to do. By then, my sister had joined us. We looked at each other, while the doctor waited.

"I cannot give that order," I said, my voice cracking. "The two of you make the decision."

My brother patted me on my arm. "We were lucky we had her all these years, Tania, but it's time to let her go."

I ran out of the hospital room, while I yelled at him, "Do whatever you need to do, just don't ask me to kill my mother. I can't do it!"

My sister ran after me, and we embraced outside my mother's room.

"My little sister," she said. She had called me that since we were children, even though I was the oldest. "I don't want our mom to die."

"Neither do I."

On his own, my brother made the decision the doctor had recommended, and we gathered the family in my mother's room to say good-bye. We were all together, the way she wanted us to be. After the doctor removed the breathing tube, she began to struggle with each breath. I could not see her like that.

"Give her more medicine, so she can relax!" I yelled at the doctors repeatedly. At one point, they told me:

"If we give her any more, the medications will kill her."

I looked at them with a blank stare.

"Isn't she already dead?"

I asked Dalia to pray out loud and ask God for my mother's eternal peace. My sister, my brother and I sat on either side of my mother and held her hands or caressed her face.

"Rest now, Mom," Gustavo said choking in his tears. "We are letting you go."

I did not want her to hear me cry, so I tried to contain my emotions. I wanted her to know that we would be fine. When her heart began to fail, and she was almost flat-lining, the nurses came in and said. "Any time now."

Suddenly, my sister let out a scream and bent over my mother's body: "No, Mom. I don't want you to go!"

The nurses could not believe what happened next. My mother's heart started to beat with more strength. She was back.

"I have never seen anything like that," said one of them.

My mother began to gasp for air, as she was doing before.

"She's suffering!" I screamed. "I don't want her to suffer."

"This is an automatic reaction. Her brain is dead," the nurse said.

But I did not believe it. I knew part of her was still there.

"Lynette, you have to let her go!" I cried. "We have to let her go. She deserves to die in peace."

"Our father, who art in Heaven . . ." whispered Dalia. She closed her eyes, held my mother's arm, and continued to pray.

Gustavo placed his arm around Lynette's back.

"Tania is right. Mom will not die in peace unless we all let her go."

My sister nodded and sobbed quietly. I approached my mother's ear and whispered:

"We will be fine, Mom. You can rest now. Don't worry."

Both my sister and my brother approached her and each said, one at a time, “We will be fine, Mom. We are ready.”

My mother’s heart began to slow down again and so did her breathing. Meanwhile, Dalia continued to pray.

As the heart-monitor line grew flatter, my eyes focused on one of the nurses. She nodded to indicate my mother’s time was near. The closer she came to the end, her face became increasingly serene, until she took her final breath.

“She is with God now,” said Dalia. “God bless her.”

One of the nurses turned off the equipment. “Sorry for your loss,” she said. “Take all the time you need.”

The nurses quietly exited the room, while my sister came around the bed and embraced me. “We lost her, my little sister,” she said.

My siblings and I caressed the arms and face of the woman who had sacrificed it all for her children. She had been a red rose against a backdrop of gray buildings, hope in the midst of chaos, kindness and love in human form. She had been our rose. Her dance had ended, but we, her children, would ensure that her spirit would go on as long as one of us lived.

***

On the night my mother died, Lynette, Gustavo, their children, and I gathered at my mother’s house. Every corner reminded us of her: the Cuban coffee she made the morning she was taken to the hospital that she had not been able to pour into her thermos, her sandals, the brown blanket I gave her for Christmas that covered her when she watched television, the numerous stuffed animals we had given her to keep her company when we worked. Her journals. One had “Tania” written on it.

Gustavo handed it to me, and later, he found others and several letters.

"These should be yours too," he said.

"She wanted you to write her story," said Lynette.

I nodded.

"I know," I replied.

I collected the journals, some of the stuffed animals, pictures of my mother and the family, and a few of the dolls I bought her during my trips to Russia, Spain, France, and Italy. She loved to collect them, so I always returned home with one.

"Let me take these to the car," I announced.

On this night of November 21, 2011, it was cool outside, but not a leaf from the massive oak tree in front of her yard moved. I put everything in the trunk of my car, and as I walked back towards her porch, exhausted, with the tension of grief upon my shoulders, something unexpected occurred. Out of nowhere, the wind began to revolve around me. Nothing else was moving, not the leaves on the oak tree or her shrubs, only chunks of my hair, as a tunnel of wind surrounded me.

Chills ran through my body. "Mom?" I said out loud, and looked up at the sky. Suddenly, the wind stopped blowing the same way it had started. I then remembered her words:

When I come to you, you will know.

At that moment, I began to weep, and later, when I managed to calm myself down, I looked up at the sky again.

"I love you, Mom," I said.

I debated whether to tell Lynette and Gustavo what had just occurred, knowing they would never believe me.

We stayed at her house for a while longer, reminiscing as we emptied her closet and began to organize her things.

"I will donate her wig to someone who has cancer," I said.

"We should donate her clothes, too," said Lynette.

"She would have liked that," said Gustavo.

Later that evening, an idea occurred to me.

I thought we should create a small partnership, owned by her three children, and move ownership of the house to it. This would allow her wishes to be fulfilled. At last, my brother and sister would have a business: "Laura Properties, LLC," — decided to call it to honor my mother. The rental income from her home would go first to satisfying her wish that each of her grandchildren receive $1,000. After that, we would use the income to help anyone in need, a grandchild, even strangers. It did not matter. Her gift would keep on giving as long as her business stayed alive, allowing her benevolent spirit to go on.

The next day, I called Lynette and Gustavo and told them my plan. They enthusiastically agreed.

I continued to work on my mother's story, but I could not touch her journals without falling apart, not for a couple of years. As my fiftieth birthday approached, I decided it was time.

What I found in her journals was invaluable. I began to rewrite her story using her own voice, and doing so allowed me to understand her like never before. I wrote feverishly, during the week, on my way to and from work as Phil drove; on weekends, as often as I could, mostly at coffee shops. It became an obsession to finish her book. I did not know exactly where I would end it. After all, I was just a medium, as often, the words flowed from my head to my hands in such an automatic fashion that it seemed like magic.

One Saturday morning, I woke up early and began to write as I typically did. The house was quiet, as Phil and I were empty-nesters. It felt lonely at times, but writing gave me a purpose.

Phil sat on a bar stool having breakfast and reading a book when I interrupted him:

"I'm finished," I said.

"Really?"

I nodded.

"After fourteen years on and off. It is finally done." I said.

"Congratulations!"

"There is something else you should know." I paused for a moment. "All this time... she knew."

"What?"

"That I would publish her story," I said, taking a deep breath. "And just today, after I finished it, I found this note. I had not seen it before. It was hiding behind a wedding picture of my parents, in the bedroom where she used to sleep when she visited."

My hands shook as I handed it to him. "To our children and grandchildren," it read:

We only ask that you love each other and your husbands or wives with the same immense love that united your father and me.

No matter what stones we found along the way, the obstacles, the unjust politics, the twelve years of separation, we stayed together until death.

This is our legacy to you. Love is the most beautiful feeling that exists in the world.

1964 – Our wedding

1997 – Year of your father's death (till death do us part)

Phil handed me the paper.

"Weird," he said.

The following weekend, when I visited my brother and sister, we uncovered another treasure hidden inside a briefcase that had belonged to my father. In it, we noticed a small white envelope. When we looked inside, we found many stamps with pieces of envelopes still attached to them. I looked at the dates on the stamps. They were all from the late 1960s and early 1970s. Then I understood.

My father had kept the stamps from my mother's letters for over twenty-five years, and our discovery of them over forty years later, as the editing of their story was in progress, made me realize they were meant to be used on the cover of their book. I also found a small Cuban flag my father had purchased when he visited Cuba; this became the background for the stamps.

In May 2015, *Waiting on Zapote Street,* my mother's story, was published, fulfilling her final wish.

And so, she would be saved one last time...

As long as someone read her story, as long as someone dared to dream, the dance of the rose would go on, forever...

The first picture was taken in Cuba, a couple of years after my father left. The second, of my mother and me, during my Sweet Fifteen celebration in Cuba. The third, of my siblings and me, was taken during my first book signing event of "Waiting on Zapote Street" in Tampa, Florida in 2015.

Collection of Testimonies

In honor of those who came to the United States from all over the world in pursuit of the American Dream. In honor of those who dared to dream. Your sacrifices paved the way for your future generations.

Acosta Family: Mr. and Mrs. Acosta and their two children left Cuba in 1968 through Varadero on a "Vuelos de la Libertad" Pan American flight to Miami. They wanted to live in a free country. The Acosta family honors Ricardo Acosta, Miriam Q. Acosta (previously Miriam Quintero González), Miriam de Los Angeles Acosta Quintero (daughter), and Ricardo Francisco Acosta Quintero (son).

Felix Acosta Dominguez: Felix left Cuba in 1992 with his wife and four-year-old son, Jarry Robertson Acosta. He was a political prisoner in Cuba who came to the United States through an agreement between the two countries.

Marilyn Alvarez: Marilyn's parents, Roger and Rafaelina Alvarez, left Havana in 1965 as part of "Vuelos de la Libertad." Marilyn honors her parents for tracing the path of freedom and opportunity for their future generations.

Victorino Alvarez: Victorino was born in the province of Camagüey, Cuba, and worked as a manager of Macareño Sugar Company, a job that allowed him to give his family a good life. That is, until 1959, when Castro's revolution triumphed and the land Victorino had inherited from his father was confiscated by the new government. He dreamed of the day he could live in a free country again. One of his daughters and his grandson left Cuba in 1968, but Victorino and his wife still had another daughter in Cuba. She and her husband were killed in an automobile accident.

Eventually, Madeline Viamontes, the daughter who had traveled to the United States in 1968, claimed Victorino and his wife. They arrived in Tampa in November 1993. His happiness was palpable from the moment he arrived. At last, after over thirty years, he was able to taste freedom again—a very emotional experience for him.

Victorino passed away in his sleep only three months after his arrival to freedom.

Graciela Beatriz Acuña (author): Graciela and her parents immigrated to the United States from Argentina in 1968. Her father had been trying to obtain visas since 1957 when Graciela was five. He first traveled to the United States alone. Six months later, his family joined him. Her father became very successful in the United States. She owes her parents everything she has.

Jose Bello: In 1959, Fidel Castro's revolution triumphed. In 1962, Jose's maternal grandmother, who had six children, began the process of obtaining visas for two of her sons: Jose's father, the oldest, and Jose's uncle. Both sons were married and had small children. In 1967, the travel visas for Jose's father arrived, and he and his wife left with their two small children (Ana and Jose). The family was allowed to bring only a few items of clothes on their flight from Camagüey to Havana, aboard a small propeller plane.

From Havana, they flew to Miami, where they spent three days at Freedom House. After being outfitted with winter-style clothing, the family flew to Chicago, their final destination, where Jose's aunt and her family lived. Jose's family underwent a culture shock, after coming from a tropical island and arriving in Chicago on February 14, 1967, in the dead of winter, unable to speak English, and with two children under five. Although Jose's mother had been an accountant in Cuba and his father, a truck driver, the couple found jobs at a packing company. Ten years later, the family moved to Tampa, Florida, and purchased a home there.

Jose's father passed away in 1991. However, his children and grandchildren now continue to enjoy the American Dream he left Cuba for.

Teresa Bonnin: *Find under Teresa Garcia Jorge.*

Norma Camero Reno: Norma immigrated to the United States from El Tigre, Venezuela. Her country, like Cuba, has been devastated by a socialist government. She left Venezuela thirty-seven years ago and came to the United States to seek a better life for herself and her daughters. An example of the American Dream, with a master's degree in international law and international business from Stetson University, Norma worked with her late husband to raise and educate their daughters in the United States.

While still in Venezuela, at the root of the socialist transformation under the Castro-Chavista regime, she found it necessary to begin the struggle for her homeland by helping groups of students who were defending it. She also created the MOVE Foundation (Organized Movement of Venezuelans Abroad) and began to send food and medicines to her people, an effort that started when her country was under the oppressive government of Hugo Chávez and has continued through now, under Nicolás Maduro. She has joined other organizations to continue sending aid to Venezuela and to work for the recovery of democracy and freedom there. To this day, her struggle continues as she writes to U.S. representatives and senators and makes trips to the U.S. Congress to raise awareness about the political and economic situation of Venezuelans. She believes that her efforts are beginning to yield fruit, as, little by little, the United States has been punishing the henchmen of the Castro-Madurista regime. Norma will continue her fight, as she anxiously awaits the day Venezuela will be free again.

Jackie Chalarca: Jackie Chalarca immigrated to the United States from Medellin, Columbia, in 1986. Her husband, Jose Gallegos, emigrated from Buenos Aires, Argentina in 1990. The couple married in New York. Jackie completed graduate studies at St. Leo University, and her husband became a certified master mechanic. They live in Valrico, Florida and have a son, who graduated from the University of Central Florida in 2016. According to Jackie, being in the United States has been the most challenging but rewarding experience of her lifetime.

Giovanny Chalarca: Giovanny came from Medellin, Colombia, in 2013. Immigrating to the United States has been a great experience for him. It has allowed him to become acquainted with a new culture and to value the differences. But even more important to Giovanny has been his ability to set goals and accomplish dreams that he might not have been able to accomplish in Colombia.

Cherian Family: Originally from India, the Cherian family—husband, wife, and three young daughters, Cheryl, Christina, and Karen—came to the United States on March 19, 1999, on a multiple-entry-visit visa. Mr. and Mrs. Cherian had been working in Dubai prior to their trip. During their visit, the family met with an immigration attorney to discuss their intent to obtain permanent residency in the United States. After considering various options, Mr. Cherian returned to Dubai, and the couple's youngest daughter was sent to India with an aunt. Mrs. Cherian remained in the United States with their ten- and seven-year-old daughters and began to attend college. Mrs. Cherian and her daughters had to travel back and forth from Dubai to the United States to ensure the family maintained their legal status. Mr. Cherian's goal was to support his wife and daughters from abroad until the family obtained permanent U.S. residency.

During the time that Mrs. Cherian stayed in the United States, she and her daughters lived in low-income housing. With no Social Security numbers, no insurance, no GPS, no cell phone, no computer, no television, and no credit, the family struggled. The children had to go to the public library to use the computer for homework assignments, and they watched television at a neighbor's house. The horrible events of September 11, 2001, delayed the family's immigration process.

After receiving her work permit and completing her BSN, Mrs. Cherian obtained employment at a Tampa hospital and went on to pursue a master's degree. Her husband, who had to travel to the United States on multiple occasions, had to resign from his position in Dubai, as his employer was no longer able to extend his leave of absence. In 2003, after receiving his work permit, Mr. Cherian obtained a position as an IT analyst at the same Tampa hospital where his wife worked.

Eventually, all the Cherian girls graduated from Hillsborough High School as valedictorians, with GPAs that exceeded 8.0. Two of them went on to become physicians, and one is finishing her master's in mental-health counseling.

The Cherians now own a few rental properties in Tampa.

The family is proud to have achieved the American Dream through hard work and sacrifice.

Cindy Chindanusorn (previously Cindy Wells): Cindy's mother, Diep Nguyen, was thirty-seven years old on September 27, 1989, when she and her four young daughters left their native home of Hue, Vietnam, to come to the United States in search of a better life and opportunity. Diep had never attended school and did not speak English, but her will to survive and her love for her children pushed her to do what was necessary. Diep met Jerry in November 1989, and gave her daughters a stepfather shortly after. She took the girls to collect cans from dumpsters around the neighborhood to help her new husband–who owned a small sign business–make ends meet.

Cindy and her family lived in the projects until her teen years. Through their persistence, hard work, and natural intelligence, her mother and stepfather had several successful business ventures, from a restaurant and a farm to a nail salon. Her stepfather passed away in 2007, and her mother, who is sixty-five now and retired, lives with Cindy, her husband, and their nineteen-month-old son.

Cindy was the first person in her family to graduate from college. She owes everything to this strong woman, who, despite hardships, despite starting with nothing, did everything she could to create a better life for herself and her children.

Ramon Docobo: Ray Docobo's father, Ramon F. Docobo, immigrated to Tampa, Florida, from Ribadeo, a Spanish province of Lugo in Galicia, Spain, in 1959. A physician in Spain, he had to work as an orderly for nearly a year before sending for his wife, Ramona V. Docobo, and their two sons. In February 1960, the family was reunited in Tampa, Florida. Eventually, Ramon was able to once again work as a physician, and he did so for years until his retirement. He and his wife had two more sons in Tampa, where the entire family still resides.

Lissette Farinas: Lissette came to the United States in search of freedom in 1995 on a direct flight from Havana. She lives in Miami, Florida with her family.

Maria Fernandez: Maria, her husband, Mario, and their two young daughters left Cuba via Costa Rica in 1983. Her family was subject to acts of repudiation in 1980 after her sister left Cuba with her family. Maria, an architect, and her husband, an engineer, lost their professional jobs. Maria bought guavas on the black market and made guava marmalade for a living, while Mario worked by picking up trash when, after 125,000 people left in 1980 through the Mariel boatlift, the trash began to pile up on the streets. Later, he worked at a park cutting weeds with a machete.

In the United States, the family prospered. Mario received his board certification and had a successful engineering-consulting business until he retired. Both of their daughters completed graduate studies in Orlando (one is a CPA and the other is an engineer).

Patricia Ford Gonzalez: Patricia honors her father, Fernando Gonzalez, from Spain, who came to the United States in 1916. Upon arrival, he first worked in the cigar industry. When he was in his late twenties, he opened a bakery with six partners. The bakery eventually failed and he returned to the cigar factory. He always loved his native country and returned to Spain often to bring clothing and other goods to his relatives. Although he never mastered English, he managed to communicate with the few words he knew. Fernando was a good, decent man who loved his family. He passed away at the age of 68.

Teresa García Jorge (now Teresa Bonin): Teresa was supposed to leave through Camarioca in 1962, but the flights out of Cuba were canceled. She eventually left on April 4, 1967, through "Vuelos de la Libertad," on a Pan Am flight. She left with her parents, Rafaela Jorge Turiño and Valerio Garcia Herrera.

Carlos Hernandez (accounting-firm partner): Carlos's grandmother, Lázara Olga Colón Martinez, was a direct descendant of Diego Colón, one of the first mayors of Puerto Rico and one of the sons of Christopher Columbus / Cristóbal Colón. Lázara and her ancestors emigrated from Puerto Rico to Cuba. Carlos's grandfather, Manuel Antonio Sed Rodriguez, and other ancestors emigrated from the Canary Islands (Spain) and France to Cuba. Manuel learned perfect English while working in New York from age eighteen through his twenties.

Lázara and Manuel met upon his return to Cuba and had three daughters. Then, on September 11, 1962, more than three years after Fidel Castro came to power, the family traveled to the United States.

While living in Cuba, Manuel had a printing shop in Santa Clara, Las Villas, Lázara's birthplace. The shop, called Imprenta Sed, was the first printing shop founded in Santa Clara. When Castro and his revolutionaries took over Cuba, the shop was confiscated, along with every personal item that belonged to Manuel. The government official told him that everything he'd owned was now government property. That was the only time Carlos's mother saw her father, Carlos's grandfather, cry.

When Manuel's family came to the United States, Lázara's first job (which did not last long) was making alterations in West Palm Beach, Florida. Her second job was as a Spanish teacher at Northboro Junior High (she had a teaching degree).

Manuel's first job was at Indian Town Printing in Indian Town, Florida. In 1965, Manuel opened his own printing business in Miami and called it "Peninsula Printing." He owned this business for many years and was able to ultimately sell it and retire. Manuel always loved the United States. Carlos's mother remembers him posting a sign in the front of his shop that read: "Si, We Speak English."

Celina Jozsi: Early in 1961, Blanca Ponte, then ten years old, assured her parents that she would care for her sister, Celina Ponte (Jozsi), who was eight years old at the time, as they left Cuba alone under the Operation Peter Pan program in order to escape communism and reach the United States. The secretive program eventually helped more than 14,000 children leave Cuba alone. Both young girls realized that they might never see their families again. In Miami, Blanca and Celina were taken to an old military camp for a month before being sent to an orphanage in Illinois for over a year.

When they were eventually reunited with their parents, they faced hunger, housing projects, and many other hardships. Both parents worked menial jobs—a stark contrast to their father's position on Cuba's Supreme Court and their mother's career as a teacher. Without a telephone or car, they walked to school and studied. They earned master's degrees, emerging from school debt free, and achieved successful careers. Celina, a college professor, has always imparted to her children, Cristina and Carlos, the importance of appreciating the true value and cost of freedom.

Moraima Labastilla Sierra: Moraima was born in Havana and became a teacher in 1956. During the Bay of Pigs Invasion, on April 17, 1961, she was arrested by Castro's communist government, then was released some time later. When she arrived in Miami in 1961, she dedicated herself to assisting over 2,000 Cubans to leave the island. In 1961, she founded and became the president of *Municipio de Güiness en el Exilio*, an organization that helped people from her birth town of Güiness who were in exile. In addition, she worked in Miami for thirty years in the Head Start program, where she performed the work of an angel by helping thousands of needy families. But she never stopped working to see her country free, not until her passing on June 12, 2005. Her three daughters, Moraima, Luly, and Madelyn, all university graduates (two of them educators), honor their mother's memory by instilling in their children, nephews, and nieces the values their mother taught them.

Clarissa Lima: In March 1980, at the age of thirteen, Clarissa Lima traveled to Spain through the plan of family reunification. She subsequently immigrated to the United States in July of that year. Clarissa graduated from the University of South Florida with a bachelor's in psychology. She currently teaches eighth-graders Intense Reading at a middle school in Tampa, Florida.

Nilda J. Llanes: Nilda came to the United States from Havana in 1999 with her husband after various unsuccessful attempts to leave Cuba. Her husband had earned a visa to travel to the United States through the lottery system.

Allen Luo: Allen came to the United States from China in 1997. He was seventeen years old nd had never been on his own before. He also did not speak English. He first lived in a high-school dormitory, then attended college and earned an MBA. Today, he works as an IT manager and lives in Tampa.

Meidy Mendoza: Meidy left Cuba on July 28, 1961, via Jamaica. She arrived in Miami on August 20, 1961.

Daisy Metz: Daisy left Colombia with her parents and two younger siblings in 1968 when she was a little girl. Her parents wanted to give their family a better future. Daisy grew up and attended school in the United States. After having three children, one of whom she lost in a tragic car accident, Daisy went back to school, while still working full time and raising her two remaining children. In 2017, Daisy graduated with a bachelor's in accounting—a difficult task to accomplish, especially after having lost a part of herself.

Pilar Ortiz: Pilar is a journalist, author, and speaker. In 1993, in Colombia—as a rookie TV reporter—she had the opportunity to cover the death of Pablo Escobar, one of the most dangerous drug dealers of all time. It was her first time live on television, and she had to overcome fear as she embraced the opportunity of a lifetime.

In 1998, after having achieved great success in Colombia, she made the decision to relocate to the United States and start from zero. She did not know anyone, did not have a job, and had to learn English, but she embraced these challenges and succeeded in her adopted country. After twenty-five years of broadcasting experience, including being the anchorwoman and the news director for eleven years at Univision Tampa (where she built the first news team ever in Spanish), Pilar created an easy-to-follow, step-by-step program called "The Speak Easy System" to help purpose-driven leaders, executives, entrepreneurs, and companies identify and deliver their message authentically and effectively so they can influence others, further their mission, and impact the world.

Pilar's book, available in Spanish and English, is *Camino al Éxito: Todos Arrancamos Aquí, (Reinventing Yourself: Creating Your Own Path to Success)*—an inspirational and powerful tool for overcoming obstacles and making powerful decisions. She began to work on the book when she was laid off from Univision Tampa due to a large reduction in staff. This major obstacle catapulted her career and her business to a new level. She decided to stay in Tampa, as she says, because "I am a proud Colombian by birth, a proud Hispanic by heritage, and a proud American by choice." Her passion is helping others to develop confidence, create their own happiness, and impact as many lives as possible.

Since 2010, Pilar has worked as a trainer, coach, international public speaker, and bilingual TV personality, motivating individuals to achieve their fullest potential in their careers and their personal lives. In 2014, she was named the Tampa Hispanic Woman of the Year. Info@PilarOrtiz.com PilarOrtiz.com (727) 557-5656.

Lina Madeline Perez: Lina and her family endured acts of repudiation in Havana, at the corner of Santos Suarez and Dureje Streets, in early 1980. Her grandfather traveled to Miami in 1981 and the rest of the family stayed in Cuba, unable to obtain jobs due to the post–Mariel boatlift discrimination against those who wanted to leave. In 1983, the family traveled to Spain. Eventually, they immigrated to the United States.

Alfredo Portomeñe: Alfredo left Cuba on October 15, 2000, worked at a hospital for many years, and retired. He lives with his children and grandchildren in Miami.

Armando Riera, RN, MSN, NP-BC: Armando emigrated from Cuba in 1980 as part of the Mariel boatlift. His goal was to seek the freedom he had lacked in his country of birth. Before he left Cuba, he had started medical school and expected to continue his studies in the United States, but life had other plans. During the treacherous journey, he became very ill, and one point even thought he would not make it. As death seemed so close, he remembered his father, who had passed away when Armando was only fourteen years old. His father had always dreamt of living in a free country. Armando knew that it was up to him to fulfill that dream as he replaced his father as head of the family.

Upon arrival in the United States, Armando began to work as a busboy at a restaurant in Miami. He then worked at a hospital as a transport assistant, while attending school to become a scrub tech. Once he had achieved that goal, the nurses in the OR encouraged him to go a step further and become a nurse. With much sacrifice and hard work he achieved that goal as well, completing his associate's, bachelor's, and master's degrees along the way. He became very active at the local, regional, and national levels as part of various professional organizations. At that point, his then boss asked him to help revitalize the Miami Chapter of the National Association of Hispanic Nurses. He accepted the challenge and has been involved ever since. Becoming involved in NAHN has afforded him the opportunity to assist Hispanic nurses and the patients they serve in the Miami community. He currently works as an adult nurse practitioner in primary care.

At last, Armando has fulfilled his father's dream of not only living in freedom and taking advantage of the opportunities it affords, but growing professionally and giving back to this great country that has given so much to him and his family.

Patsy Sánchez: Patsy was thirteen years old when she left Havana in May 1980, during the Mariel exodus. On May 15, she and her family were rescued at sea by the U.S. Coast Guard. Patsy came to Tampa, Florida, graduated from the University of South Florida, and achieved outstanding professional success. Due to her work in the community, she was recognized as Hispanic Woman of the Year in 2016 by the Tampa Bay Heritage, Inc.

Betty Viamontes (author): I am adding myself to the list to honor my mother, Milagros Valdes. Born in Cuba on the 4th of July in 1939, she was the granddaughter of Spanish immigrants. Her mother, Angela, was ahead of her time. When it was not common for women to study, Angela became a high-fashion dressmaker in Cuba and instilled in her two daughters the importance of an education. Thanks to my grandmother, my mother and my aunt went on to become university graduates. When my mother met my father, he was a manager at a window factory in Havana. They were married more than a year later, after first being very good friends for a while, and were then blessed with three children, but their lives quickly unraveled following the birth of their last child.

My father left Cuba in 1968 when I was three years old; my sister, Lissette (Lynette in the book), was two; and our brother, Rene (Gustavo in the book), was only a few months old. The Castro government stopped allowing Cuban citizens to leave, and our family was separated for twelve years. For many of those years, my mother worked twelve hours per day and on weekends to feed her children. She collected money from grocery stores, worked as a teacher, and sold goods on the black market. Despite these hardships, she always took the time to help those less fortunate.

After spending a few days at the nightmarish concentration camp "El Mosquito," we finally left Havana on April 26, 1980, on a shrimp boat, on a night when many men, women, and children perished at sea.

Through hard work and sacrifice, my family prospered in America. My family thanks, most of all, my mother, for always believing in the promise of America, and my father, for waiting for his wife and children. We also thank my aunt and uncle for supporting my mother.

My mother's name, "Milagros," means "miracles" in English. She indeed performed miracles with her three children, despite not having my father by her side. She taught us to work hard and never give up, values we took to heart. My brother is an entrepreneur, an inventor, and a manager at a glass company. He has been featured in magazines due to his expertise. Like my mother did when we lived in Cuba, he works twelve hours a day, even on weekends, to give his four children a better life. My sister has worked at a hospital for over twenty years and assists her husband in his business. I am the corporate controller at a hospital, a CPA, a speaker, and an entrepreneur. I am also proud to have been appointed by Governor Scott to the Hillsborough Community College Board of Trustees. As a teacher, my mother always emphasized the importance of an education. My participation on this board allows me to support education in our community and to honor the woman who sacrificed it all for her children's future.

I also thank my husband, Ivan (Phil in the book), for all his support in over thirty-three years of marriage. To my son, who works as a vice president of internal audit, thank you for making your country of birth—my adopted country—proud.

Mayda Vallejos Ramírez: Mayda, her sister, and their mother came to the United States through the Mariel boatlift in 1980. She brought her five-year-old son with her, but her father was turned back by the Cuban government and told he would be allowed to leave the next day. It took eight years for the family to be reunited again. We honor Mayda and her family: Mayda Ramírez Martinez, now Mayda Vallejos Ramírez; Daisy Ramírez Martinez; María Teresa Martinez; and Mayda's five-year-old son, Erick, who all left through the Mariel exodus in 1980. Angel M. Ramírez, Mayda's father, left in 1988 on a flight from Havana to Jamaica and another flight to the United States.

Maritza Venta: Maritza left Havana, Cuba, on September 11, 1985, to travel to Panama. She finally arrived in the United States on March 17, 1988. Her father stayed in Cuba. As of the writing of this book, she has not seen him for over thirty-two years because he has not been awarded a visa. She claims she will not travel to Cuba as long as the current government remains in power.

Ciro Viamontes: Ciro left Cuba on January 29, 1962. His wife and children followed in March of that year. They were among the first fifty families to be relocated from Florida to Massachusetts. Ciro was pro-Batista, and his wife, Georgelina, was a judge. She lost her job after Castro came to power. Georgelina worked as a social worker in New York City for many years. She completed all the legal paperwork to help her relatives leave Cuba. Thanks to the sacrifices of Ciro and Georgelina, Ciro's parents, all of his brothers and sisters, and other family members eventually left Cuba.

Viamontes Family: Originally from Camagüey, Cuba, the family (Guillermo and Madeline, husband and wife; and their four-year-old son, Ivan) left Cuba in 1969 from Varadero, on a chartered flight through "Viajes de La Libertad."

During the Bay of Pigs invasion, Guillermo Viamontes was a political prisoner in Cuba for nine days. Government officials subjected him to psychological torture by opening grave-sized holes in the ground and threatening to shoot him in the head.

The family will eternally thank Ciro and Georgelina Viamontes (RIP) for helping them leave Cuba.

Nina Vazquez: Nina left Cuba in 1941 to travel to the United States, thanks to a scholarship she had won. She left Havana on a boat. She was only seventeen, and a couple was assigned to care for her. The boat took her to New Orleans, and from there, she traveled by bus to Kansas City. When she arrived at St. Mary's University (previously St. Mary's College), no one spoke Spanish, and she did not speak English. The people in Kansas knew very little about Cuba, and after she was able to learn some English, the students would ask her many questions. She was invited often to their homes for dinner, as they were very interested in her story.

World War II was in full swing as she was attending college. She graduated with a bachelor's in music. From Kansas, she moved to Miami, where she met her first husband when she was playing the piano at a Miami Beach hotel. The couple married and had a son, but her husband passed away when she was still in her twenties.

She continued to play the piano and met her second husband in the City of Miami. He was the manager of the hotel where she worked. The couple had three children. Nina was tired of working at night, so she and her husband decided to leave Miami and move to Tampa, where his family lived. Nina attended the University of Tampa and trained to become an elementary-school teacher. Her second husband passed away when she was in her fifties, over forty years ago. She never remarried, but continued to live with her children and grandchildren in Tampa, where she still lives. She is ninety-three years old. By the time she retired, she had taught elementary-school students for twenty-six years.

Acknowledgements

I would like to thank, with all my heart, the people without whose contributions and commitment this book would not have been possible:

Maria Fernandez: My aunt, the woman who helped my mother raise me, and an invaluable resource who provided information about our lives in Cuba and what happened after we left Havana in 1980.

Cecilia Martin: For helping me promote my books and encouraging me during the writing process.

Diana Plattner: My talented editor for all her advice and support through the last couple of years.

Kayrene Kelley Smither: A reader I met on Facebook who read my first book, *Waiting on Zapote Street,* and since then has been a wonderful supporter. She has read and provided edits for the drafts of my last two books and promoted them. Kayrene, you are one of the many angels I have found on this journey. A big hug. God bless you.

Ivan Viamontes (my husband): Thank you for helping me with edits and for supporting me for over thirty years. We have been together since we were practically children. You are my friend, my confidant, and the love of my life.

Madeline Viamontes (my mother-in-law): For listening to me when I read you the Spanish version of this book when I translated it. After being in my adopted country for so many years, English has become my first language, and my Spanish has eroded through years of little use. Thank you for helping me utilize the right words.

When my mother was in the last days of her life, she told you: "Take care of my daughter." Thank you for being like a mother after she went to Heaven.

My brother, Rene, and my sister, Lissette: The most amazing people I know, and the personification of kindness and hard work. Thank you for telling your friends about Mom's books. You know how she was. Always telling everyone who would listen about what happened. Now, it is our turn to continue her work. To my sister, thank you for sharing with me what happened when I left home.

My mother, Milagros (Mily): Mom, if you are watching us, I hope we continue to make you proud. Your sacrifices were not in vain. Another one of your grandkids, Alex, my sister's oldest, will be married this year. He found a good girl. And so, the family keeps growing. And guess what? Soon, my brother will be featured in magazines once again for inventing a new product, and in 2015, I was appointed by the governor of the State of Florida to the Hillsborough Community College board of trustees. I know how much you valued education and hope to honor you through my contributions to this amazing school, which does so much for the young people in our community.

Mamá, your name means "miracles," and when I see all of the things your children have accomplished, I know that it was *you* all along who was there by our side—if not in person, in spirit, guiding us, advising us, reassuring us that no matter how hard life became, the sun would shine the next day. Your journey, true to your name, was full of miracles. Thank you for teaching us that life is worth living.

My readers: An author is nothing without people who read their work. Thank you for taking the time to submit reviews and telling others about my books.

Ed Zebrowski: Another reader and a professional colleague, who dedicated his personal time to modifying the picture I took in Southern France that became the cover for *The Dance of the Rose.*

Acknowledgements

PBS and the CIA for the following articles that provided historical background for some sections of the story.

http://www.pbs.org/wgbh/pages/frontline/shows/military/etc/cron.html

http://www.pbs.org/wgbh/pages/frontline/shows/pentagon/maps/4.html

https://www.cia.gov/library/center-for-the-study-of-intelligence/csi-publications/books-and-monographs/a-cold-war-conundrum/source.htm

The Miami Herald for the following article regarding the 1980 Liberty City riot.

http://www.miamiherald.com/news/local/community/miami-dade/article77769522.html

About the Author

Betty Viamontes was born in Havana, Cuba. In 1980, at age fifteen, at the height of a massive Cuban exodus from the Port of Mariel in Havana, she immigrated to the United States with her mother and siblings. Betty Viamontes completed graduate studies at the University of South Florida and moved on to a successful career in Accounting. She also completed a Graduate Certificate in Creating Writing. She has published an autobiographical novel that continues to expand its international reach, *Waiting on Zapote Street*; an anthology of short stories and poems, *Candela's Secrets and Other Havana Stories*; and various short stories and poems that have appeared on newspapers and literary magazines. Betty Viamontes is passionate about education. She is a regular speaker at the University of South Florida and other professional organizations, and currently serves on the board of Hillsborough Community College. She is also serving as Chair of the FICPA Healthcare Conference Committee. She lives in Tampa, Florida with her husband and family.